Silverheart

By

Thomas J. Mohr

To Meetra, Michaela and Mom for helping and inspiring me to write this novel. –Thomas.

1

"Can you believe it?" said my best friend May, "our first day of high school!" We looked to our right to see our first glimpse of North Star High. My name is Margaret Korikage, I am fourteen years old, which means that I have to go to high school. "I can't wait till we start our classes," May rambled on, "wonder if we'll meet any cute boys." We got off the bus and went to our classrooms, thus began our day. The classes were long, the teachers were odd, (come to think about it, some of the students were too,) and the men were absolutely, BORING!! Thank goodness for the final bell! As we walked home, May leaned over and asked me, "What did you think of the boys?"

"Honestly," I said, "I think they're all boring."

"Why do you think that?"

"Well for starters, all the jocks are interesting in is football and beer, the popular students don't care about anybody but themselves, and on top of that the less popular students try too hard to be cool."

"And your point is?"

"My point is, they all have one common interest."

"Which is?"

"They all want a girlfriend."

"What's wrong with that?"

"What's wrong is that they just want to have sex."

"Aren't you being a little judgmental?"

"I'm just stating the facts," I told her, "all of the men at North Star High are nothing but selfish, bull-headed, sex-maniacs!!"

"Gee, thanks a lot!" said a deep voice from behind. Nervously we turned around to see a vandalized wall with a young man sitting on top of it, wearing the biggest frown I've ever seen. "And I thought girls were nothing but prissy, empty-headed man-eaters."

"Ha, ha, easy to say from up there," I told him, "why don't you come down and see how prissy this girl really is."

He stared at me for a moment, then he smirked and said, "As you wish," before jumping down.

As he walked to where we were, May turned around and grabbed me by my shoulders shouting, "Margaret, what are you doing?! Don't make him mad!!"

"Who cares if he gets mad? Serves him right for butting in like that!"

"But Margaret, what if he's a serial killer or something?!!"

"Well if he is, at least we don't have to worry about going to high school."

"Margaret!! If my parents find out that I've been murdered after the first day, they're going to be sooo-!"

Before May could finish her sentence, the man tapped on her shoulder and asked, "Um excuse me, am I interrupting?" May nodded her head and moved to the side. The man was about six-foot-two and looked like he'd weigh close to one hundred sixty pounds. His body-build was buff but not ripped, covered with a white leathery jacket, black t-shirt, dark jeans and black laceless shoes. He also had dark blond hair, blue eyes and a clean shaven face. He looked at me and said, "Judging by what I heard from your friend, I take it your name's Margaret. Is that right?"

"Uh-huh," I said to him, "It is. Margaret Korikage."

"Yeah, well listen here, Margaret," he said as he loomed over me, "not everybody's a self-absorbed sex-maniac as you made 'em out to be. There are lots of guys who could care less about having a girlfriend. Take me for instance, why would I go through all the trouble of taking care of some strange woman, when I can barely take care of myself?"

I didn't know what to say. He was right. Why would he go out of his way to impress some girl, who doesn't even appreciate what he's doing for her? He stared at me waiting for an answer, then I looked over at May and said, "Uh, May?"

"Yeah, Margaret?" she responded.

"I think we should head home now."

She let out a sigh of relief and said, "I thought you'd never ask!"

After hearing May's reaction, the man shrugged his shoulders and said with a smile, "Well I've gotta get going too, y'know. Got some errands to run in the uptown so, catch ya later."

He turned around, ran towards the wall and started to climb it. When he reached the top, he started to lean forward like he was gonna jump, but before he could, "Hey!!" I shouted, "You can't just waltz in and run off like that, you haven't even mentioned your name yet!"

He paused for a moment, turned around, then said, "It's Smith, John Smith." And he front-flipped away.

We just stared at the wall for a few minutes, then May looked over and said to me, "Margaret, was it just me, or did that guy seem to like you?"

I slapped my face and shouted, "Give me a break!"

As we started to head home, I thought to myself, "John Smith, I've got a feeling we'll see each other real soon." and then continued to follow May.

We walked together for a couple of blocks, then May and I said goodbye and went our separate ways. I walked a little while longer, until I finally reached my house, 508 Sixton Street, third house on the left. When I got to the front door, I rang the doorbell to see if anybody's home. Immediately I was greeted by my little sister Sakura, who opened the door, turned around and shouted, "Mom!! Marney's back!"

As soon as she heard my sister's announcement, my mother ran to the front door and said "Why Margaret, you've come just in time for dinner. You'd better get cleaned up dear."

"Okay Mom." I told her as I went to the bathroom. After cleaning myself up a little bit, I walked out of the bathroom and made my way to the dinner table. I sat across from Mom and Sakura, with Dad sitting at the head of the table.

"So, Margaret," my father said to me, "How was your first day of high school?"

I paused for a moment, then I told him about how 'wonderful' my first day of high school was. I talked about how bizarre the teachers were, how horrible the school lunches were, how boring the men were. And so on and so forth, until I told him about the stranger May and I met on the way home, "And then he said his name was John Smith and then he jumped away."

"Ooooooh!" exclaimed Sakura, "Marney's been talking to a stranger!"

"Ugh, give me a break!" I moaned.

"Hmm," pondered my father, "sounds like you've had quite an adventure today haven't you?"

"Mm-hmm."

"Well there's plenty more where that came from!"

"Gee, thanks Dad!"

"Well I don't know about you two," said my Mom, "but I think I'm ready to go to bed."

We turned to face the clock, it was almost time to go to bed. "You have a good point," said Dad in agreement, "it's getting late, so we should all go to bed and get some sleep."

"Margaret dear," my mother asked me, "could you please make sure that Sakura brushes her teeth? She's so irresponsible when it comes to that."

"Okay Mom," I replied. I took Sakura to the bathroom so we could brush our teeth, but when we got there, Sakura asked me why do we even have to brush our teeth this late at night, so I told her we had to brush our teeth this late at night because Mom doesn't want them to rot out of our heads, "And another thing Sakura," I told her, "you don't want to have wooden teeth, now do you?"

"Ewww, no thanks," replied my eight year old sister, "I don't wanna have wooden teeth, (I don't like termites.)"

After we brushed our teeth, I took Sakura to her room, tucked her in, and said good night. After that I went to my room upstairs, where I changed into my pajamas. Before I went to bed, I took a look at myself in the mirror. I was five foot one, had long dark purple hair, thin body-build and weighed ninety-five pounds. Oh how I hated the way I looked, how straight my hair was, how pale my skin was. I hated myself to the point of tears, crying, "I'll never find Mr. Right! I'm gonna die an old maid and nobody will care!! Nobody loves me!!!" I fell on my bed, shoved my face into one of the pillows and cried until I cried myself to sleep, hoping to dream about seeing Mr. Right's face.

2

When I woke up this morning, I hadn't dreamed about Mr. Right last night. I turned my head to face the alarm clock, the time was six thirty-one a.m. I got out of bed and walked downstairs into the kitchen to make myself a bowl of cereal. As I set my bowl down in the dining room, I noticed Dad was watching the news in the living room. Dad always watched the news before he went to work, but today the news had a very unusual report that went like, "Breaking news!! Are there really monsters loose in the city? Strange reports are coming in about damaged property that may have been the work of some hideous creature; Jack Michaels has the story, Jack?"

"Good morning Erick, things have gotten a little shaky around here, but don't take my word for it, you can see for yourself the damage caused by someone, or something."

He went on to report about mysterious claw marks and giant footprints that damaged various buildings, "And where did you say the damages took place, Jack?" asked the anchorman, Erick Woodworth.

The reporter paused for a moment, then he said, "The damages took place in the uptown area, sir."

Immediately after hearing that last sentence, I dropped my spoon on the table and nearly gagged. *Did he just say the uptown area?* Then it dawned on me, 'he' was going to the uptown area when he said, "Well I've gotta get going too, y'know. Got some errands to run in the uptown so, catch ya later." *Could he be the one responsible for the damages?*

Meanwhile, Dad just scoffed saying, "Monsters wrecked those buildings? Give me a break!" And then he walked into the kitchen. After preparing his breakfast he entered the dining room, and noticed me staring blankly at the television with my spoon on the table. "Excuse me, young lady," he said to me.

"Hmm?" I replied half noticing.

"Your cereal's getting soggy."

"Oh, sorry." I said reaching for my spoon.

"Anyway, you saw that report, didn't you?"

"Mm-hm," I replied with my mouth full.

"Well, don't worry about it," he said as I continued eating, "someone just vandalized those buildings hoping to scare somebody."

I swallowed my food, then said, "You're probably right," even though the damages looked convincing.

"I'm glad you agree with me," said Dad with a smile. "Just don't tell Sakura about it, you know how gullible she is."

"I won't Dad," I said smiling back as we ate our breakfast.

When we finished eating, Mom got out of bed and walked into the dining room saying, "Good morning. How are my two favorite people in the whole wide world doing?"

"We're doing fine," we replied.

"Good." said Mom, then she turned to Dad and said, "Was there anything on the news this morning, dear?"

"Nope, just some rumors about monsters in the city," said Dad sternly.

"Monsters?!"

"But don't worry about it," Dad told her, "it's probably the work of vandals, right Margaret?"

"Right Dad," I said to him, "it probably is."

Mom let out a sigh of relief and said, "Well I hate to be a party pooper but don't you two have places to be in a few minutes?"

We turned to face the clock. It was almost time to leave. Immediately we jumped up and ran toward our separate bathrooms. I went to my bathroom upstairs, where I got a quick shower, brushed my teeth and changed my clothes. After that, I went to my room so I could get my school bag and be on my way. Then I went downstairs and as I walked toward the front door, I turned around to say goodbye to my family and then walked toward the bus stop. On my way there, I couldn't stop thinking about the news report and its contents, like the damaged buildings, bizarre claw marks and the number one suspect I think is responsible for then. When I got there, the bus had just started to pull in, meaning I had shown up just in time. As I climbed on the bus, who should greet me but my best friend May. I ran over to where she was sitting, and as I sat down next to her, we asked each other the same question at the same time, "Did you watch the news report?! Yes I did! Wait you too?!"

"Cut it out May," I said to her, "you know how annoying it is when you do that."

"Sorry Margaret," May replied, "I'm just a little nervous after watching the morning report."

"Me too."

There was a brief silence, then May asked me, "Do you think he did it?"

"Who?"

"The guy from yesterday, do you think he's the one responsible for the damages?"

All I could say is, "It's possible."

"Well he did say he was going to the uptown area, so yeah, it's possible."

"But I doubt we'll see him again," I said with a sigh, "it's not like he's gonna show up for class."

"I wouldn't be so sure about it Margaret," May said with a smile as we reached our destination.

As the bus made a complete stop, we stood up, walked out, entered the building and then separated to our classrooms. My classmates and I had Algebra as our first class, all eleven of us were there. We sat in our desks and we talked and talked, until our teacher, Mrs. Jackson, started our class with a little announcement that went like, "Good morning class, I hope you all had a good night sleep last night. Anyway, before we start Algebra, I would like to make a few announcements. First of all, I would like to thank all of you for your cooperation on yesterday's quiz, on which I think you all did a wonderful job, and I would especially like to thank Percy Anderson for having the highest score, thank you Percy."

"You're welcome," he responded.

"Yes, and second of all, Amy I know you're busy with cheerleading and all, but I'm afraid I'm going to have to fail you. Come see me after class, all right?"

"Yes ma'am." she said with a frown.

"And last but not least, some of you have been complaining about not hearing what I said and missing important details. But don't worry, I hired a note taker last night to write down what I say, so if any of you have a question about what you need to do, go ask him, I'm sure he'd give you a hand." Before she could say another word, someone knocked on the door asking to come in, so she said, "Of course, come on in, don't be shy." As the door opened Mrs. Jackson said, "Ladies and gentlemen, allow me to introduce you to your note taker."

When the note taker entered the room, I couldn't believe my eyes. It was John Smith! He was wearing the exact same clothes he wore yesterday. As I stared at him, May leaned over and whispered, "See? I told you we haven't seen the last of him."

"Gee," I told her, "why couldn't you just say, 'I told you so?'"

"I just did." She said with a smirk.

3

While we were gossiping, John was introducing himself to the other classmates, "Hello there," he said to them, "my name's John. I'll be your note-taker from now on. So if any of you have a question about what the old lady just said, bring it to me; I'm sure you'll get an answer."

After he said that, Mrs. Jackson looked at him, then she said, "John, would you please take a seat?" Even though she was probably thinking, *old lady, really?*

"Glad to," he replied.

"Good," said Mrs. Jackson, "just sit anywhere you like, dear."

He nodded his head then he paced the floor looking for a seat. While he was scanning the room, he noticed an empty desk behind May and me, and as he walked over to it, he overheard what we were saying about him. "I'm telling you Margaret," May said to me, "he's got a thing for you!"

"A thing?!" I responded, "We only met him yesterday for Pete's sake!"

"Then why hasn't he been able to keep his eyes off you?"

"Umm," I replied trying to think of an answer.

"I'll tell you why." John said out of the blue, "It's because there's not much else to look at."

"Oh what am I, chopped liver?" said Amy from a distance, and then things went downhill from there. All of the girls suddenly wanted to know why would a handsome man like him be interested in a Plain Jane like me.

Before it could get out of hand, Mrs. Jackson shouted, "Class! We are here to learn about Algebra, not to criticize John's love life. So I suggest that you all sit down, be quiet and listen, understand?"

"Yes ma'am," said my classmates.

John looked at Mrs. Jackson and said with a smile, "Couldn't have said it better myself." And then he sat down in the empty desk behind May and me. The lesson was about division, something I've never been good at, and as we were studying, John tapped me on the shoulder and whispered, "Hey, I got your name, but I never got your friend's name over there, what is it?"

"It's May," I told him.

"May what?"

"May Ai."

John stared at me for a moment, then he asked me, "You're kidding right?"

"Nope, it really is, May Ai."

"How do you spell that?"

"M-A-Y, A-I."

"Is there something you'd like to tell us Miss Korikage?" Mrs. Jackson said to me. Apparently she noticed I was talking about something that had nothing to do with the lesson.

"No, Mrs. Jackson, there isn't." I sheepishly told her.

She glared at me for a moment, then she said, "Then I better not hear you talking about something that has nothing to do with the lesson, understand?"

I nodded my head, and then she returned to the lesson. Now having the information that he needed, John leaned over and whispered, "May Ai, gotcha."

"Just do your job," I told him, and then he remained silent for the rest of class. John actually seemed very good at note taking. It looked like he copied down everything Mrs. Jackson said, right down to the last period. But he was behind me, so I couldn't know. After a few minutes, the bell rang. We grabbed our textbooks, and left her classroom. Our next class was history, and you'll never guess who was there. Apparently Mrs. Jackson didn't hire John just to take notes for her class, she hired him for all of our classes.

At lunch, May and I began to wonder, why did Mrs. Jackson hire John to take notes for all our classes, and is John the one responsible for the damages on the news report? But as we were looking for a place to sit, I noticed John was sitting across from Percy Anderson, who seemed to be looking at May in a sort of romantic way. Realizing this, John tapped him on the shoulder and said, "Go on, say something to 'em"

Percy nodded his head, and then said, "Uh, Margaret?"

"Yeah?" I responded.

"Would you and May like to sit with us?"

I paused for a moment, then I said, "Sure, we would love to."

Percy smiled and said, "WAHOO!! I mean, thank you."

I smiled back, then May and I put our trays on the table, and sat down. Percy is five foot four, and weighs close to two hundred pounds. He also has green eyes, black hair, and a chubby body build. Percy has always had a crush on May ever since kindergarten. Unfortunately she never noticed him, and he's also very shy. As for May, she's five foot two and a half, and weighs ninety-four pounds. Also, she has orange hair, blue eyes, and a thin body build. May has always been into romance for as far back as I can remember. But she just can't seem to find the right guy, and she has to wear glasses too. I sat next to John, and May sat next to Percy. Neither one of us spoke, until I said, "So, did you guys see the news report this morning?"

"Oh boy, did I?" said Percy, "I've still got the Goosebumps to show for it!"

John's response however was, "Didn't need to."

"Why?" I said to him.

He shrugged his shoulders, then said, "'Cause I was there."

As soon as he said that, May let out a gasp then said, "So you ARE the one who di-!"

"Hold it," John said after he grabbed May's mouth, "I said I was there, I never said I DID anything while I was there, understand?"

May nodded her head, and then he let go of her mouth. "Your hand tastes like tap water," she said to him.

He just smiled and said, "I try."

I cleared my throat, then asked him, "Then why were you there?"

"I was grocery shopping," John told me. "My refrigerator was empty, so I had to buy food uptown. I was on my way there, when I happened to hear what you said about the guys here."

"What did she say?" said a wide eyed Percy.

"I'll tell you." John said to him.

"Don't you dare." I told him, knowing fully well what I said yesterday.

Ignoring every word I said, John told Percy, "She said all of the guys at North Star High are nothing but selfish, bull-headed, sex-maniacs. Do you agree?"

"No not completely," said Percy, "although it describes Brent pretty well, it doesn't describe me at all." Immediately after he said that, I thought of his crush on May, and then started to giggle. "Uh, did I just say something funny?" he said as I continued giggling.

"Oh, it's nothing," I said trying hard not to laugh, "nothing at all."

"Well," said May, "if you didn't do the damages, who did?"

After hearing that, John smiled and said, "Maybe it was one of those monsters."

"You can't seriously believe that, can you?" I said to him, "That's crazy!"

"It may be crazy," he replied, but then again, the truth is often crazier than a lie sometimes, am I right?"

"I guess so," I said half stunned by his answer.

"Anyway," he said as he grabbed his fork, "I'm done talking, can we eat now?"

Percy responded, "I thought you'd never ask!" And then we ate our lunch.

As soon as we finished, the bell rang, and we headed for class. Our next three classes came and went, until the last bell. As May and I left the building, Percy asked if he could walk home with us, so I said, "Sure, we could use a big strong man like you." And that was it.

A few blocks later, Percy asked us, "So, where do you girls live?"

"508 Sixton Street," I told him, "it's the one on the left,"

"The third house on the left, got it." He said, "And where do you live, May?"

She paused for a moment, then she said, "I live over on Johnston Avenue."

"Really?" said Percy, "Which house?"

"The one close to the middle, it's on the left side."

Percy gasped after hearing those words, and then he smiled and said, "It's funny, I happen to live a few houses across from there."

"Far out!" said May, "We're practically neighbors!" And then she and Percy started to laugh.

They continued to laugh and chat for the next few blocks, until we reached Johnston Avenue, where we said good bye to each other and went our separate ways. When they left, I felt my heart sink. "I'm alone again," I sighed, "As usual." I dragged my feet the whole way home, and as I reached my house, I said to myself, "I wonder how everybody else's day went."

When I knocked on the front door, Sakura came up to it and asked me, "What's the secret password?"

"Let me in, and I won't hurt you." I said to her.

"Close enough," she said as she opened the door.

After Sakura let me in, Mom came out of the kitchen with her apron on and said, "Margaret, I'm so glad you're home!"

"Me too, Mom," I said to her, "how was your day?"

"Couldn't have been better," she said, "How was yours?"

"You would not believe who showed up at school today."

"Dinner's almost ready. You can tell me about it after you wash up, okay?"

"Okay Mom." I said to her, and then I went straight to the bathroom. After I washed my face, I left the bathroom and made my way to the dining room, where my family was sitting there waiting for me.

"Don't just stand there," said my dad, "take a seat, talk to us, and tell us how your day went."

"Okay, Dad." I replied. Then I told them about my day. I started with my walk to the bus station and ended with my walk home. But when I got to the part about the new note-taker, well, "And when he walked through the door, I couldn't believe my eyes, it was John Smith!"

"The man from yesterday?" Mom said, "Why would he do that?"

"I think it might've been something I said," I told her.

"If that's true," my dad responded, "you must've made quite an impression on him."

"I don't think that's it," I said to him.

Sakura gasped, then said, "He's a stalker Marny, he's gotta be!"

"A stalker?!" I responded.

"And that's enough from the peanut gallery," said Mom as she grabbed Sakura's mouth. "Let's eat now!"

Dad and I nodded our heads, and then we ate our dinner. After we finished our meal, I stood up, thanked Mom for the food, and went upstairs to brush my teeth. While I was doing that, I couldn't stop thinking about what John had said at lunch, "The truth is often crazier than a lie." What did he mean by that?

But as I pondered this, Dad walked in and said, "Do you mind if I join you?"

"Not at all," I said with my mouth full of toothpaste, "Come on in, I'm almost done anyway."

"Thank you, my dear," he said as he reached for his toothbrush, "it's a pleasure to brush my teeth alongside a young lady like you."

I giggled, then spat out the toothpaste and said, "Dad?"

"Hmm?"

"Any news about the damages?" I asked as I rinsed out my toothbrush.

He paused for a moment, then said, "Nothing we don't already know."

"Okay."

"Don't worry about it," Dad said as I rinsed my mouth out with water, "it's like I said this morning, someone just vandalized those buildings hoping to scare somebody."

After he said that, I gurgled, then spat out the water and said, "Maybe you're right." And then I said good night to him, and left the bathroom. When I entered my room, I changed into my pajamas and flopped on my bed. As I lay there, I thought about how the other girls called me a Plain Jane, and how they've treated me over the years. They've mocked me, they've teased me, they've even hurt me both physically and emotionally. I started to cry when I thought about Sakura and her wonderful social life. Sakura's never been lonely, she has at least a dozen friends from school; in fact, she's made eleven friends over the summer. But as for me, there's only one person I can call friend after so many years. With that, I burst into tears and shoved my face into one of the pillows, where I cried until I fell asleep.

4

Two weeks have passed since the second day of high school, it's now Saturday morning at seven a.m. I was still asleep, when somebody called our house phone. Half dazed, I got out of bed, walked over to the nearest phone and said, "Hello?"

"Rise and shine sleeping beauty!" said an all too familiar voice.

"May! What are you doing calling me this early in the morning?!"

"Sounds like you're all bright eyed and bushy tailed this morning." she said with a cheerful tone of voice.

"Ha, ha, ha." I replied," Very funny, now why are you calling me, May?"

"I'm calling to see if I can come over. I already asked my parents about it and they said it was okay!"

"Come over? Here?"

"That's right, I thought that since I haven't been over to your house in a while, and the fact that you sound like you could use a friend, it'll be perfect! What'da say?"

I paused for a moment, then I said, "Well, I think I'd need to ask my parents first."

As soon as I said that, Dad walked out of his and Mom's bedroom with a phone in his hands and said, "No need, I heard everything you said May, you have my permission to come over."

"Dad!" I said to him.

"Mr. K!" said May, "I-I had no idea that-."

"It's alright," Dad told her, "No one's in any trouble, right Margaret?"

"I guess so." I responded.

"And besides," he said to May, "I already gave you my permission, you just need Margaret's."

After he said that, May asked me, "Well, what do you say Margaret, can I come over?"

I paused for a moment, then I smiled and said, "Of course you can May, you're always welcome here!"

"That's great! When can I come over?"

"How about this afternoon at three o'clock?"

"That's perfect Margaret! I'll see you then!"

"Looking forward to it," I said to her, "bye!"

"Bye Margaret, bye Mr. K!" she said to Dad and me.

"Sayonara Miss Ai." said Dad, as we hung up our phones.

After that, I went to the kitchen downstairs to make myself a bowl of cereal for breakfast. Dad did the same thing, and as we were eating, Mom came downstairs and asked Dad, "Who was that on the phone?"

"It was just May," he responded, "She asked us if she could come over."

"What did you say to her?"

"I said yes," he told her, "but it was Margaret who told her if she could come over."

"I see." Mom said to him, then she turned towards me and said, "Margaret, what are your and May's plans for this afternoon?"

"Nothing much," I said to her, "we'll probably just hang around and talk to each other, nothing special."

Mom stared at me for a moment, then she said, "Alright dear, I just wanted to know what your plans were."

"Okay Mom." and then we ate out breakfast.

Sakura didn't wake up until after we finished our breakfast, and when she entered the dining room, she asked Mom, "Where's my breakfast?"

"Well, what do you want for breakfast?" Mom said to her.

"Ice cream!"

"How about a bowl of cereal instead?"

"That too!" said Sakura, and that was it.

Sakura is four feet tall and weighs forty one pounds. She also has pink hair, grey eyes and a thin body build. As for my parents, my mother is forty years old, five foot four, and weighs one hundred thirty one pounds, with pink hair, blue eyes, and a thin body build. While my father's forty two years old, six feet tall, one hundred fifty pounds, purple hair, grey eyes, and a thin body. They have been married for sixteen years, and have only two children, me and Sakura. Dad works at an office, while Mom stays at home. People have told me I have my mother's eyes, and my father's lavender hair. But anyway, I went upstairs to get a shower and brush my teeth. After I did those things, I put on a T-shirt and shorts, then I went to my room, where I did my homework and waited for May. A few hours later, Mom called me down for lunch, and as I walked down stairs, someone was knocking on the door. I walked over to the door to see who it was, and when I opened it, who should I see but my best friend May, holding a pair of suite cases. "Hi Margaret!" she said to me.

"Hi May," I responded, "gosh, you're early."

"Better that than late, I always say."

"When have you ever said that?"

"I just did," she said with a smile, and then we started to laugh.

"Hey, we're about to have lunch, would you care to join us?"

"Aw, I would love to, but I already had lunch at my house so I guess I'll just set up shop, okay?"

"Alright, be my guest." I told her, then I joined my family in the dining room, while May unpacked her things in my room.

When I entered the dining room, Mom asked me, "Sweetie, who was that at the door?"

"Just May," I told her, "She came by early."

"Well, did she want to eat with us?"

"No ma'am, May already ate before she left her house."

"I guess she didn't want a sandwich," Dad said with a hint of disappointment in his eyes.

"Don't worry dear," Mom said to him, "it's her loss, not yours."

"You're right, but personally, I wouldn't blame her if I'd known THIS is what we'd be having for lunch."

"Hey, don't talk like that. You make wonderful sandwiches, right girls?"

"Right Mom!" I told her.

While Sakura just frowned and said, "I like Mommy's better." And then we ate our lunch.

A little while later, May walked into the kitchen and said, "Hi everybody, I'm here!"

Immediately after she said that, Sakura jumped out of her seat, and ran towards May shouting, "Minmei, you're here!!"

"Yep, didn't I just say that?"

"Uh huh," Sakura said as she hugged May, "you sure did."

"Miss Ai," Dad joined in, "you're even more beautiful in person."

"Thank you," she said to him, "it's nice to see you too Mr. K."

"The pleasure's all mine," he said with a bow.

Mom cleared her throat, then she said, "Hello May, how are your parents doing?"

"They're doing great," May told her, "thanks for asking."

"You're welcome."

"Anyways," May said as she turned towards me, " came down here to tell you that I've got everything set up and I'm just waiting for you to come upstairs. What do you say?"

I paused for a moment, then I said, "Yeah, let's do it!"

"Alrighty," she said while grabbing my hand, "it's girl time!" and then we ran upstairs.

When we got to my room, the makeup and nail polish kits were there waiting for us. "Should you go first," I said, "or shall I?"

"Who said anything about taking turns?" May said to me, "We're old enough to put makeup on ourselves!"

"Of course, I was planning on doing that anyway. I was talking about the nails when I said that."

"If it's about the nails, then I guess I'll go first since I am the guest after all."

"Okay, it's a deal!" and then we got down to business.

After I finished doing May's fingernails, she started to do mine, and as she was doing them, she asked me, "So, what do you think of high school so far?"

I frowned, then said with a sigh, "So far, I think it's depressing."

"Why do you think that?"

"I think that because if you look around, the only things anybody wants to talk about are having sex, drinking beer, and smoking dope. For example, I saw Brent and Amy make out in the bleachers not too long ago."

"Ew, really?"

"Yeah, another example would be that last week, some of the students got arrested for underage drinking and possessing marijuana."

"That's terrible."

"And that's not the worst of it, some of the older students are pregnant, and even a few of them have at least one child or two."

"Aw, cheer up Margaret. Not everybody's like that. I know I'm a hopeless romantic and all, but I'm not THAT gross about it, right?"

I nodded my head, then I said, "That's true."

"And Percy," she continued, "he's not perfect, but he's a sweet guy."

"Especially when it comes to you," I said while trying hard not to giggle.

"What?"

"Oh never mind."

"You know, Percy's not the only one who's sweet."

"What are you suggesting?"

May took in a deep breath, then she said, "What I'm suggesting is that there are other sweet guys around here."

"Like who?"

"Like John."

"John?! Don't even get me started on him!"

"Why not?" she said as I started to laugh.

"I'll tell you why not," I told her, "first of all, he treats me like a child. Second, he doesn't want us to use his last name or even tell anybody about it."

"Why not?"

"He didn't say. And third, we don't know anything about him, and when I try to bring it up, he'll just say, 'You wouldn't believe me if I told you.'"

"I'm sure he'll tell us when he's ready."

"For your sake, I hope you're right. He's hiding something I just know it."

"And for the finishing touch... There, all done!"

I looked at my finger nails and saw what May had done. She had clipped them, filed them, and topped it all off with Royal Purple nail polish to match my hair. "Wow, they look beautiful."

"Uh huh," she responded, "and I did the same thing with your toe nails, not that anyone will see them but, I think they look nice."

"Gosh, I don't know what to say."

"Don't sell yourself short my friend." She told me, "You also did a great job on my nails too, see?"

She showed me her nails, and I don't mean to brag, but she was right, I did do a great job. I did the exact same thing she did with my nails, except that I used Peppy Pink nail polish instead of Royal Purple, and I did them much faster than she did mine, too. "You know, I think you're right May."

"Of course I am Margaret, that's what friends are for. Now grab that lipstick and eyeliner, and let's get pretty shall we?"

"Oh let's!" I responded, and we grabbed the makeup kit, and ran toward the bathroom. When we got there, we put down the makeup kit, then we picked out what we were going to use, and then we started to put it all on. While we were doing that, I asked May, "So, what do you think of Percy?"

"S'cuse me?" she responded.

"You said he was a sweet guy. Does that mean you like him?"

"Well, I like him as a friend, but I don't think of him in a romantic way or anything. Why do you ask?"

"Um," I said while trying hard not to laugh, "no reason, I was just wondering what you thought of him, that's all."

"Okay!" she said to me, as we continued to put on our makeup.

When the two of us finished, we turned to look at each other's handiwork, and when we looked at our faces, we giggled, then said to each other, "You look beautiful! Hey, that's my line."
And then we started to laugh.

I used Dark Lavender eyeliner, while May used Radiant Pink, but we both used Pearl Pink lipstick. While we were laughing, Mom and Sakura walked in, with Mom saying, "Girls, do you want pizza for dinner?"

"Yes ma'am!" we responded.

"Good," Mom said, "just make sure you wash your faces before dinner."

"Aw," I said to her, "but Mom."

"No buts," she replied, "you two look like a pair of clowns, and I don't think pizza would go to well with that makeup, alright?"

"Okay Mom," I replied, "you win."

"Good, see you at dinner." and then she left the bathroom.

After she left, Sakura came up and asked us, "Could you do me next?"

May and I looked at each other for a moment, then we nodded our heads, and I said, "Of course, we'd just LOVE to make you look pretty."

And then we did Sakura's face. When we finished, May and I left the bathroom and entered my room. "I don't know about you Margaret," May told me, "but I had fun putting makeup on Sakura."

"Really?" I replied, "So did I!"

"Do you think you mom will get mad at us for putting makeup on Sakura?"

"Not a chance. If anything, Mom'll think she looks ten years older."

"Wow, your mom must really love your sister."

"May my dear friend, you have no idea." And we started to laugh.

After we did that, May said, "Hey, let's see what's on TV, okay Margaret?"

"Okay, why not?"

"Alright then," May said as she grabbed the remote, "Let's watch some Sci-Fi!" But when she turned on the television, it wasn't the usual programing, but an urgent news report that would leave us baffled.

5

"What the...?!" May said as it started, "This isn't the Space Soldier marathon, it's just a news report."

"Wait, don't change the channel," I told her, "I want to see this."

It started like the way it normally would, except that the anchorman Erick Woodworth had a very different emergency to report, "Breaking news!! This just in, turns out that the damages from two weeks ago, may not have been done by some blubbering behemoth. Recent damages show that it could've been the work of a vandal trying to terrorize the people of North Star. Jack Michaels has the story, Jack?"

"Good afternoon Erick, you may remember earlier reports suggesting that monsters were behind this, turns out this may not be the case. Two weeks ago in the uptown area, an unexplained phenomenon occurred, giant foot prints and mysterious claw marks were found on various buildings. The damages were severe, but no one was injured, leaving us scratching our heads. But today, we found similar damages in the south side area, that may give us a clue as to who did this and why."

When the reporter finished speaking, it then showed a shrewd looking man with a beard and wearing dark sunglasses pointing at a damaged wall saying, "These incisions were made by a steel sword, not a pair of giant claws."

"Dan Smith," the reporter continued, "a crime scene investigator, says that these damages were nothing out of the ordinary at all, but rather common vandalism done by a single individual hoping to terrorize the good people of North Star."

"This wasn't done by monsters," said the shrewd man, "there's just no such things."

"How do you know that?"

"Because I'm an expert, I've seen things like this all the time, this was definitely vandalism."

"How can you prove it?"

The shrewd man took in a deep breath, then said, "I can prove it because I found this at the scene of the crime."

After he said that, he pulled out an evidence bag with a piece of white leathery cloth inside it. When I saw it, I almost gagged. Could that be a piece of John's jacket, or somebody else's? I didn't know. But when the reporter saw it, he said, "Are you sure about it, because isn't that circumstantial evidence?"

"Could be," the shrewd man replied, "but I believe it gives us a clue as to who did this, and why."

"We still don't have a plausible suspect at this time Erick," he said to the anchorman, "but the investigation is ongoing, so don't expect anything real soon. For all of you at home, this is Jack Michaels for channel eight news, now back to your usual programming." The very second after he said that, the reporter jumped up and said, "Yes, finally! This could be the story of the year! I'm going to be famous, I'll become an anchorman, I may even get a news show of my own! It's Jack time, Woo!" and then he started to dance.

While he was doing a thigh thrust, someone shouted, "Jack! You're still on the air, you doofus!"

After that, the reporter turned towards the camera with a sheepish grin on his face, and said, "Heh heh, oops." And then it switched to Space Soldier.

May laughed for a moment, then she said, "Who says there's nothing good on the news, eh Margaret?"

"True, but never mind that. Did you see what that guy passed off as evidence?"

"Yeah, what about it?"

"It was a piece of white leathery cloth, now how many people do we know who wear that kind of material?"

"Margaret, are you suggesting John's the one behind this whole mess?"

"I'm not suggesting anything, I'm just saying he might be."

"Yeah, but you know that guy did say it was circumstantial evidence."

"Well I guess that's true."

"Uh-huh, it also could've been from somebody else's jacket, you know."

"Good point May. And there's no way we can prove John was there either."

"Exactly, so can we please stop talking about John, and watch Space Soldier now?

I paused for a second, then I said, "Okay sure! I was getting tired of talking about him anyway." And then we giggled, and started to watch Space Soldier.

We watched only one episode of the marathon, when May asked me, "Margaret, which do you think is weirder, that fact that this show is based off a drawing, or that Percy's been staring at us through your window over there?"

"WHAT?!" I responded, "Since when?"

"Since I came here," she told me, "he followed me."

"And you had to wait till just now to tell me?!" she nodded her head, then I said, "Where is he?"

"Out that window over there." She responded, and then I looked out the window and saw Percy, holding a pair of binoculars, standing near the left side of our thorn bush. "How should we deal with him Margaret?"

"I'll distract him while you sneak out from the back and catch him by surprise." I told her.

"Rodger." She replied, and she walked downstairs.

While May was doing that, I opened the window, and said, "Hi Percy!"

As soon as I said that, Percy looked up and said, "Oh, hi Margaret!"

"What'cha doing with those binoculars?"

"Oh, these? I was just doing a little bird watching."

"From my house?"

He paused for a moment, then he said, "Yeah, you have prettier birds here, than where I live. Speaking of pretty birds, you look very cute with that makeup on."

"Thank you," I said while slightly giggling.

"So, where's May?"

"She's in the bathroom, would you like me to leave her a message?"

"Yeah, tell her that I want to see her when she gets out, okay?"

"Alright, anything else?"

"Yeah, I'd also like you to tell her…" And then he made a list of things to tell May when she left the bathroom. But as he was making it, May walked over to his left side, (fortunately, he didn't notice her.) And when he finished, he asked me, "Do you think you can remember all that?"

"Gee," I replied, "that's quite a mouthful, I think you'd better tell her yourself."

After I said that, Percy turned to his left, where he saw May standing almost right on top of him saying, "Hi Percy!"

"Yeeagh!!!" He shouted, and dived into the thorn bush.

After he did that, I said, "Oh my gosh! Don't move, I'll be right down!" and then I ran downstairs.

When I got outside, I went over to where Percy and May were, and as I saw Percy lying there, I couldn't help but giggle. "How did I do Margaret?" May asked me.

"Like a true professional," I told her, "although I didn't think he'd actually jump into the thorn bush like that."

"Neither did I. I feel like we need to apologize, don't you?"

"I'll say."

We turned towards Percy and said, "Percy, we're sorry for making you jump into the thorn bush like that, will you please forgive us?"

"Aw, you guys don't have to apologize," he replied, "I'm the one who needs to apologize."

"Oh we forgive you," May said to him, "right Margaret?"

"Right," I replied, "if you really wanted to come over, you should've asked."

Percy made a big sheepish grin, and said, "Guess I should've, I forgive you guys. Now can you help me up please?"

May and I looked at each other, nodded our heads, and said, "Sure, we'd be happy to!" and then we helped him up.

Percy was covered in thorns, (which is not too surprising.) And as we pulled them out, he asked me, "Margaret, do you think your parents will get mad at me for ruining that thorn bush?"

"Probably not," I told him, "that thorn bush has been around since I was little, and it's caused nothing but trouble since it stood there."

"Wow, really?"

"Yeah. So in a way, you just did us a big favor."

"Gosh, I feel so honored."

I giggled, then said, "I'm glad you do, now hold still." as I pulled out another thorn.

May and I kept pulling out thorns, until Dad came out and asked us, "So, what have you done to my thorn bush?"

"Gee Dad," I said to him, "do you have to ask?"

"Nope, I just heard a scream, and wanted to know if you and May were okay, that's all."

"We're fine Dad, that scream you heard was Percy over there."

Dad nodded his head, and he said, "I see, and what is he doing here?"

"He followed May here, and he's been staring at us through my window with a pair of binoculars ever since he got here."

After hearing this, Dad turned towards Percy and said, "Young man, is it true what my daughter just said?"

"Every word of it." Percy said with a sigh.

"I should call your parents about this," Dad said to him, "but it looks like you've been punished enough, right girls?" May and I nodded our heads, then he continued to say, "So I won't call them, but I will leave you with a warning. Don't mess with my girls."

"I know," Percy replied, "I found that out the hard way."

"Good," Dad said, "now let's get you patched up. I can't send you home bleeding like that, can I?"

"No sir."

"Oh, and as for you two..." Dad said to us, "My wife loves what you did with Sakura, you two made her look ten years older."

"Told ya." I whispered to May, and then we all went inside.

While Dad took care of Percy, May and I went upstairs to wash the makeup off our faces. When we were finished doing that, Mom came up and told us, "Girls, the pizza's here!"

"Okay Mom!" I replied.

"By the way, whose idea was it to put makeup on Sakura anyway?"

"It was both of ours Mrs. K," May told her. "We thought it'd be fun to make her look cute like us, y'know?"

"Well, I would like to tell you two that I love what you did with her. But I can see that my husband already told you girls, didn't he?"

"Yes, he did Mom," I told her.

"So there's no real need to repeat myself, is there?"

"No ma'am." We responded, then we started to laugh.

As we were doing that, Mom said, "Well girls, I'll be downstairs. Don't stay up here too long or we'll eat without you."

"We're coming Mom," I said to her, "don't rush us."

"Wouldn't dream of it." Mom said, and then we went downstairs.

When we got there, Percy was gone, and Dad was in the dining room with Sakura and the pizza. "Good evening ladies", Dad said to us, "for your dining pleasure we have one hand-tossed pepperoni pizza, five bread sticks, and a liter of coke for refreshment."

"Oh, you," Mom said and then they kissed.

We sat down, put a slice of pizza on each of our plates, and we started to eat. A little while later, Dad asked us, "So did any of you see the news report this afternoon?"

"May and I did," I responded. "Why do you ask?"

"Because it proves that monsters weren't the ones responsible for the damages. I was right!"

"Is that the only reason you're mentioning it dear?" Mom asked him.

Dad paused for a second, then he said, "Sort of, I just thought I'd tell the girls, so they'd stop worrying about it. Haven't I told them there are no such things as monsters?"

"Yes," Mom told him, "You did, several times in fact."

"Exactly," Dad continued as he turned towards May and me, "but for now I'd like to hear what you two have to say about it."

"I didn't like the investigator very much," I told Dad, "he just looks shady to me. And I don't think he presented the evidence very well either."

"Good point Margaret," Dad said to me, then he turned towards May and said, "Do you have anything to say on the report, Miss Ai?"

"Well I'd kind of have to agree with Margaret Mr. K," May said to him, "that one guy didn't present the evidence very well."

"I see," Dad said, "anything else?"

"Yeah," May replied, "it also made Margaret think that someone from our school is the one responsible for the damages."

"Really, who?"

"I won't say who it is," May told him, "but honestly, I don't think he'd do something like that, right Margaret?"

I wanted to disagree with her, but I said, "Right May, he couldn't have. Now can we please stop talking about the damages?"

"I couldn't agree more, dear." Mom said, and then we moved on.

We continued to talk for a while, then we had some dessert. After that, May and I got up, thanked Mom and Dad for dinner, and went upstairs to brush our teeth. When we were finished doing that, we went into my room where we changed into our pajamas. Afterwards, I asked May, "Where do you want to sleep tonight?"

"Oh, anywhere will do," she said.

"Did you bring your sleeping bag?"

"Can't say that I have," she said after shaking her head.

"I'll get the mattress," I told her, then I pulled the mattress in question out from under my bed. "Did you bring some pillows and a blanket?"

"Of course I did Margaret, how else am I going to sleep around here?" And then she pulled out two pillows and a blanket from one of her suitcases. After she did that, we said good night to each other, then I turned off the lights, and we went to bed. As I lay in my bed, I started to think that what if John IS the one responsible for the damages on the news? Could he really be capable of doing something like that, or could somebody else have done it? I didn't know. Also, I thought about Mr. Right. Will I ever see his face, or will it remain forever a mystery? With that, I broke down and started crying. I must've been crying louder than I thought, because a few minutes later, May got up, tapped me on my right shoulder, and said, "Margaret, why are you crying?"

I wept for a moment, then I turned towards her saying, "What if I never see Mr. Right's face, May? How will I survive?"

"Like you've always have Margaret, it's not the end of the world."

"Sure feels like it."

"Calm down. Sometimes having a man in your life isn't always the best thing for you, y'know?"

"What's your point May?"

She sat down next to me, then she said, "My point is that maybe you shouldn't worry about stuff like this. I'm sure you'll find your prince charming someday."

I slightly giggled after she said that, then I wiped the tears off my face, and said "May, you've spoken like a true romantic."

"I know, it's a gift." And then we hugged each other.

As we did that I said, "Thank you May."

"Anytime Margaret," May responded, "that's what best friends are for." Then she got up, lay back down, and we went to sleep.

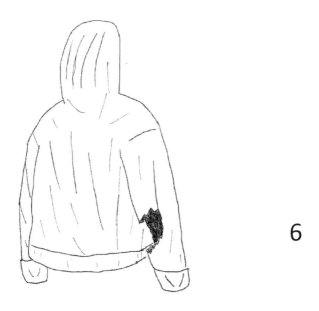

6

The next day, I woke up at six twenty in the morning, just as the sun was barely starting to rise. When I got out of bed, I tiptoed past May, who was still sleeping. I went downstairs to make myself some breakfast. After I ate a bowl of cereal, I went to the bathroom where I washed my face, changed into the clothes I had on yesterday, and brushed my teeth. When I finished doing those things, I put my hair in a ponytail, and then I went to the front door, put on a pair of socks and tennis shoes. I ran outside for a Sunday morning jog. I like to jog on days like this, the fresh air, the wind in my face, and even the sweat I get from doing it. I ran for a while, until I reached Pennington Street, where I heard, "Come on man, put your back into it!"

It didn't take long for me to realize it was John's voice. Then I turned my head to the right and saw where it came from. It came from a large white four story mansion. Pennington Street is reserved for only the richest people in North Star. "John

Smith, a millionaire?" I thought to myself. Of course that was a little hard to swallow, so I decided to go in and investigate.

I knocked on the front door three times, but no one answered. So I tried turning the doorknob. It wasn't locked. Then I opened the door and went inside. I couldn't believe how beautiful it was on the inside, I saw paintings, sculptures, vases and many other things that would cost more than my house. I made my way to the back yard pool and sure enough, I saw where the noise came from. John was lying down on a lounge chair without his jacket, while Percy, (A.K.A. the one he was yelling at,) was doing push-ups, wearing a bathing suit and covered in bandages. After he did eleven of them, Percy flopped on his face saying, "John, can I please get in the water now?"

"Who told you to stop?!" John replied, "Get up!" Then Percy went back to what he was doing. "Seriously, what am I gonna do with-?" John looked up and saw me standing behind the glass door. Then he smiled and said, "So, The Thorned Rose pays me a visit. How cute."

"Thorned Rose?" I asked as I opened the glass door and walked towards the pool, "Where did that come from?"

"You don't remember? Percy told me about how you and your friend made him jump into a thorn bush."

"He did, didn't he?" John nodded his head. "So, this is where you live."

"Yep, it's all mine. At least while my parents are away."

"I see."

"Hey, what's with the t-shirt and shorts? I thought you'd be wearing that uniform like you always do."

"Do you really think I'd wear my nice clothes on a morning jog? You're crazy."

"No, what's crazy is the fact that it's an improvement."

"Hey!" What I usually wear is a white short sleeved shirt, (long sleeved if it's cold,) purple knee socks, black lace less dress shoes and a purple plaid skirt and tie. A minute or two later, I said, "John?"

"Yeah?"

"Are you going to let Percy get in the water?"

"Why should I? He's fine."

"Really? 'Cause he looks like he's about to pass out."

John didn't reply. He turned toward Percy and told him, "Alright, you can get in now."

Percy jumped to his feet. "Really?!" he asked. John nodded his head. Then he turned around crouched down and shouted, "Cowabunga!!" As he cannonballed into the pool.

When he did, Percy managed to splash water all over me. All on my clothes, my hair, EVERYWHERE! "Aww, Percy!" I moaned, "Ugh!!"

"Man," John said, (of course he didn't get a single drop on him,) "you got soaked didn't ya?"

"Uh-huh…"

"Come here." Then he put his arm around my wet shoulders saying, "Let's get you dried off." And then he led me inside.

John took me to a powder room upstairs. He gave me a towel and a bathrobe, then he told me to wait there while he went to get me some dry clothes. After he left, I dried myself off and changed out of my wet clothes. After that, I sneaked around for a little bit to see if John really lived there. I looked in just about every room, and I didn't see anything that said otherwise. Until, I opened a door to one of the broom closets and saw John's jacket, hanging from a hook with a hole in the right elbow. I took it down to get a closer look. It looked like that piece of cloth from the news would fit in it perfectly. Then, knowing John would be back any minute, I ran to the nearest phone and called 911. "911," said a woman's voice, "what's your emergency?"

"Yes, I think I know who's responsible for the damages."

"Could you please tell me your name, miss?"

"What? No, that's not important right now!"

"Could you at least tell me where you're at?"

"Well, uh… I'm in a mansion on Pennington Street."

"Can you tell me the house number?"

Crud! I forgot to look! "I don't know."

"Then can you go outside and see?"

"Well, I can't do that either."

"And why not?"

"Because I don't have any clothes on!"

There was an awkward silence. "I'm sorry ma'am, there's nothing I can do for you."

"No, wait! I'm wearing a bath-!" Then she hung up, "Robe."

And just when I thought things couldn't get any worse, "Margaret," John said from behind, "who were you talking to?"

"John!" I shouted as I turned around and dropped the phone, "I-I-I was talking to May when-."

"Don't lie to me. I know who you were really talking to."

"Y-you do?"

"Yes I do. You think I'm the one responsible for the damages because you saw a hole in my jacket that looks like that piece of cloth on the news. Am I right, or wrong?"

What was I supposed to say? He was right. Instead I asked him, "Then how did you get that hole in your jacket?"

He froze for a moment, then he replied, "I had a little pest control problem a while back, when my jacket got caught in one of the doors. Does that answer your question?"

"Uh... Yeah, yeah it does."

We both went silent. Then John handed me a pink silk-like dress, a pair of white boots, pink socks with black stripes and a pink bandana. "These were my cousin's," he told me, "Try them on, I bet you'd look cute in them."

"No, I don't think-."

"Come on, you'll look great. Trust me." Then he left the room and closed the door behind him.

I knew better than to look a gift horse in the mouth, so I put on everything John gave me, I even wrapped the bandana over the top of my head, (which wasn't really necessary.) After I bow tied the ties on the back of the dress, John knocked on the door. I told him he could come in, then he opened the door and walked in. When he saw me, he was nearly speechless. "I told you I'd look ridiculous in these."

"No," he replied, "far from it. You're beautiful." Then he took my hand saying, "Come on and see for yourself." And we left that room. It was a little awkward walking around in those boots, I definitely hadn't broke them in yet. John led me to a bedroom with a mirror. When he showed me my reflection, he asked, "What do you think?"

I couldn't believe it, for once I actually looked... Girly. Before I knew it, I started to giggle. Then I began to pose and saw myself in different angles. "Wow," I said, "thank you."

"No problem, it's not every day I get to supply clothes to a beautiful young woman."

I couldn't help but laugh when he said that. "Well, I'll be heading home now." After that I curtsied. Then John responded with a bow and that was it. I grabbed my wet clothes, went downstairs, and left the mansion. I walked home instead of running, I was in no rush. I even skipped a little bit, (don't ask me why.) "May was right," I thought the whole way, "he IS nice!" When I made it home I knocked on the door and called out, "Hellooo! Anybody home?"

A few seconds later, May opened the door and saw me in my borrowed clothes. "Whoa!!" she said as her eyes widened, "Margaret, what happened to you?!"

"You mean the outfit? John gave it to me when-."

"No, that goofy grin."

"Huh? I'm... Grinning?"

"Yeah, I've never seen you like this. Are you okay?"

"I'm fine, in fact I've never felt better."

"Obviously." Then we started to laugh. Next, May turned to her left and shouted, "Hey everyone, come look at this!"

Before I knew it, my whole family went to the front door. When they saw me, they were in total awe. After I spun around, Dad said, "WOW. Young lady, do you have any plans tonight?"

Mom elbowed him in the chest, then she told me, "You look lovely sweetheart."

And last but not least, Sakura asked, "Who are you and what have you done to my sister?"

"I'll take that as a complement, little 'sis," I replied with a giggle. Then I noticed May had her suitcases at her sides. "Are you leaving?"

"Yep," May replied, "afraid so. I wish I could stay longer, but my parents will kill me if I'm any later than one."

"Oh well, it was nice having you over, May."

"Same here. It's what best friends do after all. See you tomorrow."

"You too, bye!" And then we hugged each other before May picked up her suit cases and walked home. After she left, I went upstairs to my room. But when I flopped down on my bed, I felt something in the dress pinch me. I pulled it out and saw what it was. It was a price tag. The dress was twenty dollars and it had today's date on it. I knew what it meant. John didn't get it from his cousin, he must've ran to the nearest clothing shop and picked out a dress he thought would look cute on me. And I bet he did the same thing for the rest of the outfit. All the same, I smiled and said, "John, you're sweet." I spent the rest of the day thinking about John and how I couldn't wait to see him tomorrow, knowing all too well, I would.

7

The next month was possibly the happiest time of my life. I didn't cry at all, my grades were at their peak and I spent nearly every spare minute I had with John. I walked home with him, I visited his house whenever I could, and I even bought him a new jacket. It was perfect. Until today came, then everything took a turn for the worse. Yesterday, Mrs. Jackson and the other teachers thought it'd be a great idea to have a pool party before it got cold. They decided to have it at John's mansion early in the afternoon. I asked John why he told them about his house, and he said, "I'm sorry Margaret, they practically squeezed it out of me."

Of course I forgave John, so long as I got to be with him, I didn't care. After I had breakfast, showered and brushed my teeth, I put on the clothes he gave me and left the house. By the time I got there, his house was packed. And when I say packed, I mean PACKED. I walked up to the front door and walked in. After I walked past the foyer and opened the back door, I saw a couple of girls in bikinis, a few boys splashing around in the pool and some of the teachers talking from a corner. But I didn't see John. "Funny," I thought to myself, "I wonder why he's not here. Maybe he's upstairs 'cause of the noise?"

"Well, well, well," said a girl I knew all too well from behind, "Plain Jane Korikage thinks she's a princess. Shall we break the news to her?"

"Go away Amy," I replied as I turned to face her and her friends, "can't you leave me alone?"

"I don't take orders from you, Korikage. Besides, it's my job to put losers like you in their place."

"I don't have to listen to-." Then two of Amy's friends grabbed me by my arms. "H-hey! Let me go or I'll-!"

"My oh my, that's a pretty outfit," then she pulled out a bottle of permanent ink and said, "It'd be a shame if something were to HAPPEN to it."

"Stop, Stop it please!" Then she opened the bottle and began to pour it all over my dress and boots. When the damage was done, they started to laugh as I fell to my knees crying, "No... No!!" And that wasn't the worst of it. Next they stood me up while Amy took a few steps back. Then she started to run at me full speed. I knew what was coming next, so I tried to struggle and break free. But by the time I got them to let go of me, it was too late. Amy jumped up, kicked me in my chest and then I fell into the pool. I nearly blacked out. But just before I could, I saw someone jump in, grab hold of me, and pull me out. As he carried me to the nearest lounge chair, I looked up at him and said, "John Smith?"

He looked back at me replying, "Who's John Smith?" Then he set me down and sat next to me. I was slightly confused by his answer, how could he not know who John is? He's in my class! Meanwhile, I noticed the pool had turned slightly black and the teachers were yelling at Amy. I didn't hear what they were saying, but I didn't need to, their body language told me everything I needed to know. Needless to say, it ended with Amy leaving in a huff. "Looks like they're finally giving her the axe." Then I looked towards him and he said, "By the way my name's-."

"Jarred, Jarred Maddison." I replied.

"How do know my name?"

"I remembered you from kindergarten. You were always so quiet, so shy."

"Heh, guess I still am." Then we laughed a little bit, until I sneezed. "Oh, you must be chilly. I'll get you a towel."

After he came back and I dried off a little bit, I asked, "Jarred?"

"Hmm?"

"What did you mean when you said, 'who's John Smith?'"

He paused, then he said, "I don't know who you're talking about.

"Uh, John Smith. You know, the note taker?"

"No, I think you're mistaken."

"Huh?"

"You must be talking about John Jones, that's his name."

What?! He thinks his last name's Jones?! I didn't want to believe it, I hoped with all my heart that he made a mistake. But it didn't stop there. Another Student came out and said, "Jones? Get real! It's Evans, that's it!"

And another one replied, "You've gotta be kidding, it's John James!"

"You all lose," shouted one of the weirder students, "it's clearly John D. Baptist!!" And so on and so forth.

As the argument escalated, I started to feel faint. All those false names, all those lies... It was more than I could take. So I stood up and walked toward the exit. But when I entered the foyer, John was standing right in front of me with a smile saying, "Hi Margaret!" Those two words stopped me right in my tracks. Then he looked at Amy's handiwork and said with wide eyes, "Whoa, what happened to your clothes?!" I didn't reply. "What's that noise in the back? What are they shouting about?!" I didn't speak. There was a brief silence, then he started to look worried, "Margaret, is something wrong?"

After that, I looked him in the eyes as tears ran down my cheeks, "How could you?!! I trusted you, I believed everything you said, I even wore this dress for you! And now I've found out you've lied to everyone from the start! You've lied to my teachers, you've lied to my friends, and you've lied to me! I almost drowned in your pool, because I'm wearing these stupid clothes! And that noise you're hearing, is the sound of everyone at North Star High, trying to figure out which name, if any, is yours! How's that for wrong?!!"

Right then and there, John ran up to me and grabbed my mouth. His face was white with horror, as if every word I said stabbed his heart. "Not here," he told me, then he walked towards the stairs saying, "Follow me." And I did as he said.

He led me to a room with a balcony on the top floor. And after he closed the door, I asked, "John, what is going on?"

"I can't tell you."

"Why not?"

"Because I don't want you involved."

"Why, who are you?"

He paused for a moment, then he leaned on the railings, and said, "Are you familiar with the damages on the news?"

"Yes, why do you ask? Are you the one responsible for them?"

"In a way, sort of."

"Sort of, what do you mean by that?!"

"Calm down. I'm asking you because... Do you believe monsters exist?"

"What kind of question is that? Of course I don't!" I told him, then I felt a chill run up my spine, compelling me to ask him, "Do you?"

He paused for a moment, then he looked at me and said with a straight face, "Yes, I do."

"Y-you, you can't be serious can you?"

"I'm sorry to say this, but I am. The monsters on the news are very real and dangerous, and it's my job to take care of them before they become a threat to innocent people, like you."

I paused for a moment, then I said with that same chill running through my whole body now, "T... That's insane... I don't believe you!"

"I was afraid you'd say that," he said with a frown, then suddenly, he jumped up on the edge of the building, turned around, and said, "Margaret, I didn't want to do this, but you leave me no other choice. It's time for you to wake up, and face reality!" And then he leaned back, and fell off the balcony.

I ran over to where he was standing, and then I looked down and saw him hit the sidewalk with a... Splash?! I couldn't believe it, John turned into a puddle of water when he hit the ground!! And the next thing I saw was the puddle of water disappearing as he climbed out of it. I was so scared, I didn't know what to think. So I ran downstairs, screaming at the top of my lungs, until I got to the first floor, where I fell, hit my head, and then blacked out.

8

When I woke up, I was in the hospital, lying down on the cot,

with gauze wrapped around my forehead. I also noticed a nurse was there too. The nurse was talking on the phone with someone, while a janitor was sitting down in one of the chairs. I felt like it was time for me to go, so I decided to get up and walk out. But as I started to get up, I felt a burning pain in my head, then I yelled out, and started to cry a little. "What was that noise you ask?" said the nurse to whoever it was on the phone, "Oh she just woke up, your daughter did hit her head pretty hard you know. Now how soon can you get here?... Uh huh?... Five minutes?... Good, then I'll see you when you get here... Okay, bye bye." After she hung up the phone, she turned towards me and said, "You are one lucky girl, Miss Korikage. That little fall of yours could've given you a concussion."

"Thanks but," I said to her, "who was that on the phone? Ow..."

"That was your father, sweetheart. He said he'll pick you up in about five minutes."

"That's good," I said with a groan. Then I sat up and asked the nurse, "So, if I don't have a concussion, then why do I have gauze wrapped around my forehead?"

"Because there's a small cut on it. Don't worry, it's nothing serious. However you will have a bruise there for quite a while."

"Just my luck."

"By the way, what were you screaming about when you fell?"

"I was screaming because I saw-!" And then I remembered seeing John fall off the balcony, and transform into a puddle of water when he hit the sidewalk.

"Well," said the nurse waiting for an answer, "what did you see?"

Knowing she wouldn't believe me, I told her, "Oh, it might've been nothing, I probably just imagined it."

"That doesn't answer the question. What did you see?"

"I don't wanna talk about it," I said while putting my hand on my forehead, "My head's killing me."

"Then maybe you should lie down, Miss Korikage."

"I think I will. By the way, thank you for taking care of me."

"It was my pleasure sweetie, I am a nurse after all." And then I laid down, and waited for Dad.

As I lay there, I thought about asking her how I got in the hospital. But before I could, Dad walked into the hospital room saying, "Hey Mrs. Mcgillacutty, how's my little lady doing?"

"Great, she's been a real trooper," she told him, "she only has a small cut and a bruise, she'll live."

"That's good to hear." Then he turned towards me and said, "Well, I see you've gotten yourself a red badge of courage, eh?"

"Very funny Dad," I replied, "can we please leave now?"

"I couldn't agree more my dear, do you need me to carry you?"

"No, I can walk. Just barely."

"Alright then," he said as I got out of the cot, "We'll be off. Thank you Mrs. Mcgillacutty for taking care of my daughter."

"It's no trouble, I am a nurse after all," she responded, and then we left the hospital.

After we left the building, Dad and I walked over to his car parked out front. As he unlocked it, he asked me, "Do you want to sit up front with me, Kitty?"

"No thanks Dad," I replied, "I'd rather lie down in the back seat if you don't mind."

"Suit yourself," said Dad with a chuckle, and then we got inside, and drove off.

A few miles down the road, I asked Dad, "So, how was your day at work Dad?"

"Nah, can't complain." He responded, "It was like any other day, long and predictable. But what about yours, did anything happen at school today Margaret?"

I paused for a moment, then I took a deep breath and said, "It all started when..." And then I told him everything that happened today, from what Amy did to me, to John's last name game. But when I got to the part about the balcony, "And then he leaned back, and fell off the balcony."

"He fell off the balcony, why would he do that?"

"I don't know Dad. But when I ran over to where he was standing, and saw him hit the sidewalk, he... Oh..."

"What's wrong Kitty? You seem to be crying."

"Dad..." I said while trying to regain my composure, "Promise me you won't laugh when I tell you what happened next."

"Laugh, why would I laugh? I believe you so far."

"Promise me Dad."

He paused for a moment, then he said, "Okay sweetie, I promise."

"Alright, here it goes. When he hit the sidewalk he... He turned into a puddle of water." Right after I said that, Dad chuckled slightly from the front seat. "You promised!"

"Sorry, it's just a little crazy for me."

"It gets crazier Dad. The puddle of water started to disappear when John climbed out of it."

"Now I know you're making it up."

"Dad!"

"You must've hit your head harder than I thought."

"I'm not making this up!"

"Calm down, you probably just dreamed it up when you hit your head, that's all."

"But Dad, I didn't-!"

"Margaret!" He shouted, then he calmed down and said, "Look, I know you want me to believe you and all that, but there's no way I can believe that this John Smith or whatever his name is turned into a puddle of water after falling from a four story building. So just drop it and move on, okay?"

I paused for a moment, then I broke down and said, "Fine, you don't believe me anyway." And then I began to cry.

When we got to the house, Dad climbed out of the car, opened the back door on the left side and said, "We're home now sweetie. Do you want me to carry you now?"

I just cried for a moment, then I nodded my head and said, "Just take me to my room please? I don't feel like eating."

"I see," he said with a sigh, "Suit yourself." And then he picked me up, and carried me into the house.

As we went inside, Mom came out from the kitchen, and said, "Oh my gosh! What happened to her?"

"Nothing, she just had a rough day at school, that's all." He told her as he carried me upstairs.

When he got to my room, he set me down on the bed, pulled the covers over me, and said, "Good night Margaret, I'll see you in the morning." And then he kissed me on the forehead, and walked out of my room.

After that, I heard Dad talk to Mom about what happened to me at school today. And when he got to the end, Mom said, "Are you sure that's what she said to you?"

"I'm positive Amanda," he told her, "she actually believed she saw this John Smith, or whatever his name is, turn into a puddle of water after he fell from a four story building."

"Oh Ken, what are we going to do?"

"I don't know dear. I want to believe her on this, but there's no way on earth I'll ever give in to such childish nonsense. So I'll just have to conclude that it was all a bad dream she had when Margaret hit her head."

"Kenji, are you trying to tell me our daughter is going insane?"

"I hope not. Look there's no reason to get worried over something that may have never happened. So let's just go downstairs and eat the food you cooked for us, okay?"

She paused for a moment, then she said, "Alright, let's do that." And then I heard them walk downstairs.

Childish nonsense, going insane?! I couldn't believe what I just heard. My parents have always supported me, time and time again. Now they seem to think of me as the little girl who cried wolf. But that was nothing compared to what I saw today. John turned into a puddle of water when he hit the sidewalk. He also told me that the monsters on the news were real and it was his job to take care of them before they get out of hand. So what does that mean, he's a monster hunter? It was crazy, but it was the only answer I could think of. That also meant there could be monsters everywhere, in jungles, in caves, even in my closet. With that in mind I rolled over, clutched one of my pillows, and said, "John, what are you and why are you here?" And then I closed my eyes and cried myself to sleep.

9

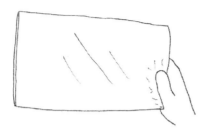

The next week at school, John was gone. Mrs. Jackson told us he left a note saying we knew too much and it was time for him to leave. She also said he never took a single note the whole time he was here, they were all blank, as if he'd done it all before. And it wasn't just in her class, all of the classes John took notes for had blank notes too. "As if he'd cheated his way to a paycheck." I heard from one of the teachers.

But if he didn't take notes, then what was he writing? I didn't know, how could I know? As the days went by, one thing led to another. At school, my grades and my friendships have been sliding. May and I haven't been talking to each other recently, namely because I've been avoiding her. Ever since John fell off the balcony, she's been nagging me about what happened there. So I tell her things like, "I don't wanna talk about it." And, "You wouldn't believe me if I told you."

And she'll say, "Now YOU'RE the one keeping secrets."

Also, May's been spending a lot of time with Percy these days, a LOT of time with Percy. I know what you're thinking, but it's true. Also, as it turned out, Amy was expelled for what she did at the pool party. But that didn't make me feel better, nor did anything else. I was too far gone. Jarred came up to me at school once and said, "Hiya Margaret!"

"What is it Jarred?" Was my reply.

"I was wondering... If you'd... You know..." Then he turned around and started mumbling to himself. I knew he wanted to ask me something, but what? "Margaret?" he said after a while.

"Yes?"

"Would you like to... Go to the winter prom with me?"

My heart practically stopped cold. Why would he ask me to go with him? How could I respond to something like that, after what I went through? "Jarred, w-why would you... Ask me?"

"Because I think we're made for each other," then he grabbed my hands and looked into my eyes, "think about it. You and I have noticed each other since childhood, and ever since then my heart beats for you. Though you couldn't hear it then, you can now. So please, open your heart and listen to the sound of my love."

I didn't say anything right away. I could've said, "Jarred of course I'll go with you. Now and forever." And fell into his arms. But instead, I told him, "Jarred, I'm sorry but I can't. You're a nice guy, really you are, but I can't go with you. My heart belongs to someone else and I just can't love you the same way I loved him. I'm sorry, but that's the way it has to be... Good bye." Then I turned around and started to walk away.

After I took a few steps, Jarred came up and grabbed my shoulder, "Margaret..."

"STAY AWAY FROM ME!!" And then I ran away from him. I could've had a happy relationship, been with someone that cared about me. But instead, I gave that up for what? Absolutely nothing. Nothing but a fantasy that's beyond my reach. I kept running until I made it outside, then I hid in the bushes and cried my heart out.

Whenever I wasn't at school, I was either in my room crying my eyes out, or at Pennington Street staring at John's mansion for hours on end. To me, that's where I could feel John the most. One day it started to rain. Did I go home? No. I was still standing there getting soaked to the skin. I had nothing better to do. Then a butler came out and saw me. "I say," he said, "what are you doing out in this weather?" I was in too deep in my thoughts to notice him. He went inside and came out with an umbrella, then he walked up to me saying, "Come inside my dear child, I shan't have you ill on my account." And he led me inside.

The butler took me to the same room where John gave me my pink dress. One of the fondest moments of my life happened here, now it was nothing but an empty room. The butler gave me a towel and some dry clothes. After I changed, a middle aged man walked in. When he saw me, he said, "Oh ho, I see you've made a friend, eh Mr. Boston?"

"Sir, this girl was standing in the deluge outside," the butler replied, "I did what any respectable gentleman would do."

"I see," the he turned towards me and asked, "And what's your name kid?"

I turned away from him. "HE used to call me kid," I thought to myself, "I miss him so much!"

"Come on," the man said, "don't be shy."

After a second or two of silence, I said, "It's Margaret."

"Margaret... Hmm... Your last name wouldn't happen to be Korikage would it?" I nodded my head. "I knew I recognized you!"

"How?"

"I never forgot. You sent me a file you made by yourself."

I giggled slightly, "I was so worried Dad would get fired that I went to your office and begged you to let him keep his job."

"And that was the sweetest thing I ever saw. I wish my daughters were more like you."

"I don't think you would, trust me."

"An honest answer, why don't we go downstairs for some tea?"

"If you insist." Then we walked to the dining room.

We sat there for a good time while Mr. Boston served us tea and dropped in every now and then. It was nice talking to the man again. His name was Mr. Boswell. "Now are you sure you don't want to keep those clothes?"

"Yeah, they're a little big on me and I don't wanna impose."

"Don't worry! My daughter never wears them, (come to think about it, she never wears half the clothes she buys.)"

"Thank you."

"Now if there's anything you'd like to ask me, ask away."

Immediately a question came to mind. "Mr. Boswell?"

"Yeah?"

"Do you know John Smith?"

He froze for a second, then he replied, "Who?"

"Maybe you know him as John Jones, or John Evans or anything like that."

"No, I can't say that I have. Who is he?"

"He's someone I met about three months ago. He said he lived here with his parents."

"Wait, HERE? In MY house?!"

"Y-yes."

"Kid, I have lived here for ten years. I was on vacation during that time. And now you're telling me some random yutz told you a story like that?! Bull! Total bull!"

"A-and the worst part was when he had a pool party over here."

All of a sudden his face turned red with fury. Then he slammed the table and shouted at the top of his lungs, "IF I EVER GET MY HANDS ON HIM, HE'S GONNA GET WHAT'S COMING!!!"

"Bwaaaaahh!!" And then I shoved my face in my arms and began crying.

No sooner then I started, Mr. Boswell calmed down and said, "I-I'm sorry, I didn't mean-."

"You did." Then the room went silent. After a minute or so I stood up saying, "I have to go."

"Can I drive you home?"

"No sir, I can walk."

"Can I have Mr. Boston walk you home?"

"I'm fine."

"Can I at least give you an umbrella?"

"Fine, if you insist sir."

After he gave me one of his daughters unused umbrellas, Mr. Boswell led me to the door. When I started to leave, he said, "You still have a big heart. I'm sorry you had to see me like that."

"I forgive you, goodbye." Then I made my way home. It was nice to smile again, if not for a brief moment. But it didn't last. When I got home, I saw the channel eight news van parked outside my house. "What's that doing here?" I thought, "Did something happen?"

As I walked toward the front door, Jack Michaels and Dan Smith left my house. "I can't believe we've hit another dead end," said the reporter to his shady partner, "we've interviewed everyone on this block!"

Before I could even set foot inside, Dan Smith grabbed my shoulder growling, "Not everyone." Then he turned me around and asked, "You, girl, what's your name?"

"M-Margaret Korikage."

"Where were you on the day of the Boswell Manor incident?"

"What?"

He shook me shouting, "Don't mess with me!"

"Dan please," Jack told him, "allow me, you're scaring her." Then he turned toward me, "We know you were at the pool party two months ago at Boswell Manor, can you tell us what happened?"

All I could say was, "I can try." I told them what happened, from the time I walked in to my time in the hospital. "And that's what happened, sir."

"Aw, I see. Thanks anyway." He turned toward his partner telling him, "Like I said, another dead end. Let's go."

"Not yet." Was Dan's reply.

"Aw, why man?"

"She's not telling us everything." He was right. I didn't tell them about John or what he did on the balcony, and I didn't want to. I tried to sneak into the house, but he turned toward me before I had the chance, "Something else happened that day, something you're not telling us. What is it?"

"I don't know what you're talking about." Was my reply.

Suddenly Dan slammed me against the front door. "Don't lie to me you little brat!! What is it, what are you hiding?!!"

"I... I... I..."

"Dan stop," Jack said to his partner, "she's had eno-."

"You shut up!" Dan, replied, "She's hiding something, I know it! I'll find it even if I have to-!"

"Fine!" I shouted with tears running down my cheeks, "I'll tell you everything!" And I did just that. I told him everything I knew about John, from the day I met him, to the days I spent at Boswell Manor. I also gave them a full description of his appearance. When I started to reach the end, I said, "He told me I needed to wake up and face reality. Then he leaned back and fell of the railings."

"So he committed suicide?" Jack asked.

"No, when he hit the ground... he..."

"Yes?" Dan said.

"He... he... oh..."

"Spit it out you little-!"

"He turned into a puddle of water!!" Then I cried in my hands.

I heard Dan chuckle, and when I looked up I saw him smiling. "We've got him."

"Huh?" Was Jack's response.

"He's our guy, get the picture?"

"Umm..."

"Let's go, I told you this wasn't a waste of time."

"Wait!" I said.

"What?"

"What will you do when you find him?"

"Why do you care?"

"Be... Because I... I..."

"Heh heh, oh I see. Come here." But when I did, he punched me in the stomach. Then he started to choke me saying, "Get this picture. If you EVER get between me and my goals, I will stomp you out with everything I've got." Even though he was wearing dark sunglasses, I could almost see a blue glow behind them. It screamed Evil. Then he threw me into one of the puddles on the front lawn. "Thanks a lot, you little cry baby," was the last thing I heard from him before he and his partner drove off.

All at once I began to cry. I told that thug John's secret. I stabbed him in the back. "Oh John... What have I done?!" was all I could say to myself.

That was three days ago. It's now Thursday evening in the winter. The bruise on my forehead is gone, but now my left eye twitches when I'm nervous, or angry. I had just walked in the front door and started to go upstairs to change into my pajamas and brush my teeth, since I wasn't hungry anyway. After I did those things, I went to my room and closed the door behind me. Then I sat down on my bed, and started to think for a minute. I thought about John, about how we met, and how he turned my world upside down. I miss him so much, his beautiful blue eyes, his easy going attitude, his annoying shaggy hair, and his dark watery secret. With that in mind, I put my hands over my face, and started to cry. "How did it all come to this? My family thinks I'm insane, my friends don't have time for me anymore, and I'm all alone. Nobody loves me!" I got up, grabbed my school bag, and then threw it at the door.

When it fell to the floor, I noticed a little white envelope fly out of my bag, then I went over to pick it up. When I opened the envelope, there was a little note inside. It read, "Dear Margaret,

I know I shouldn't be doing this, but I can't stand it anymore. Everytime I watch you suffer, every time I see you cry, every time I see a tear fall from your cheek because of me is more than I can take. Meet me at this address and I'll tell you everything. Sincerely, John."

"John?" After I finished reading it, I flipped it over and saw a map on the back of it. It didn't take long for me to notice the address John mentioned, it was circled in red ink. And when I saw where it was, I nearly gagged. John lived over on Bluebird Boulevard, the other side of town! I didn't know what to think. I almost panicked. But then I realized, this could be my only chance to find some answers, to make sense out of all this. So I made up my mind, I said to myself, "I'm going to find John."

10

When I told May my decision the next day after school, she said, "What?! Are you crazy?"

"No," I replied, "I've made up my mind. I'm going to find John."

"But this is Bluebird Boulevard you're talking about, the other side of town! You know all the bad stuff that happens there!"

"I know, but if I don't go there now, I may never find the answers I'm looking for."

"Answers? You're still obsessed over the damages, aren't you?!"

"No, this is about more than that. This is about the truth, the truth that only John knows."

"Listen to yourself Margaret, this is crazy!"

"It may be crazy, but then again the truth is often crazier than a lie."

"Don't give me that! What will your parents think if you ran away like this?"

"They think I'm insane May, they're planning to put me on medication. I have to do this."

"Drop it Margaret!" she shouted, "Just drop it! Because if you don't, then our friendship is over."

What was I supposed to do? May was my best friend, the only one I ever had. As I stared into her angry eyes, I made my decision. I paused for a moment, then I said in a weak trembling voice, "Good bye May." And then I ran away from her crying.

I kept running for a few blocks, until I got to a bench, where I sat down and cried for a while. I couldn't believe what just happened. May never yelled at me like that before, she was my best friend. Now I'm all alone, sitting on a bench, thinking about the wonderful friendship I had just given up. But it was too late for me to undo my decision. So I stood up, wiped away my tears, and headed towards Bluebird Boulevard. I got there in about two hours, and as I followed the map's instructions, they led me to a sleazy hotel called, "The Drunken Turtle."

I almost didn't want to go in, but I told myself, "It's now or never Margaret, make your move." And then I walked inside.

When I got to the front desk, I was immediately greeted by a man with red hair, green eyes, and a slender body build, who said, "Hey there little lady, what can I do for you?"

"Well um," I replied, "can you help me find John Smith?"

"Who?"

"John Smith, does he have a room here?"

"He might, what does he look like kid?"

"He has blue eyes, shaggy blond hair, and he wears a white leathery jacket all the time."

The man paused for a moment, then he smiled and said, "Gee, you must be talking about Snake Eyes."

"Snake Eyes?"

"Yeah, he's lived here for about four years now. I called him Snake Eyes 'cause he never told me his real name. Come to think about it, he never tells me anything. He's on the fifth floor, room seven eleven, you can't miss it."

"Room seven eleven, thanks!"

"Hold it young lady!" he said before I took another step, "The elevator isn't working at the moment, and I wouldn't go upstairs alone if I were you. I think I'd better take you there myself if you don't mind."

"I don't, thank you."

"Ah, it's my pleasure." And then he took me to John's room. As we approached room seven eleven, the man looked over and asked me, "Why are you so interested in 'ole Snake Eyes anyway, is he your boyfriend?"

"Boyfriend?! N-no, why would you-?"

"Just asking, I'll leave you be." And then he went downstairs.

There I was, staring at the door to John's room, wondering if he was even in there or not. I slowly walked up to the door, and knocked on it. I heard footsteps coming closer, followed by a clicking sound from the door, and before I knew it, the door opened and there he was. I barely recognized him, he wasn't wearing his jacket like he usually did, he wasn't wearing his shoes ether, and he seemed to have neglected to shave. As I stood there, he looked down at me and said, "Margaret, what are you doing here?"

I paused for a moment, then I put my hands on my hips, looked him in the eye, and said, "I came here looking for you, I want some answers John."

"Why? You saw what you saw. How did you find me anyway?"

"The envelope you gave me led me here."

"I see," he said with a sigh, "it looks like there's no escaping it, is there?"

"I guess not."

"Would you like to come in? This place gets a little rough on the weekends."

"Delighted." And then he let me in.

There's not much to say about John's room. It wasn't very big, there was hardly any furniture, (besides a single bed, armchair, small television set, and a cabinet.) And the bathroom was slightly smaller than the room itself. It was nothing like Boswell Manor. I hung my jacket on the hook behind the front door along with John's. "Please," he said, "Make yourself at home." And as I sat down on the bed, he looked at me and said, "So you came all the way out here looking for me. Why?"

"I just told you, I want some answers John."

"About what?"

"About what happened in that room two months ago."

"Like I said before, you saw what you saw. Go home."

I paused for a moment, then I told him, "I can't go home."

"Why not, won't your parents get worried about you?"

"My parents think I'm insane! Ever since I told them about what happened, they've been freezing me out of everything! They're even planning to put me on medication."

John turned towards me with a look of shock on his face. "And what about your friend May, did you tell her about what happened Margaret?"

"No, I haven't. Besides, she's my not my friend anymore."

"Why, what happened?"

"After school today, I told her I was going to find you. She thought I was still obsessed over the damages, then I said it was about more than that. Eventually she told me to either drop it, or end our friendship. And so I... I..." and then I started to cry.

"Oh, I'm so sorry."

I continued to cry, then I said, "She was my only friend. We did everything together, we played together, laughed together, and even cried together. Now I'm all alone, no friends, no family... No one."

John walked over to where I was. Then he sat down next to me, put his arms around me, and said, "I'm here. And to be honest, I actually envy you."

"Me, why?"

"You still have a family and friends. All I have is a crummy room and a horrible job."

"Why? Don't you have a family?"

He paused for a moment, then he said, "No, not anymore."

"Why? What happened?"

"Listen to me Margaret." He said as he let go of me, then he looked me in the eye and said, "This is the story you've been waiting to hear."

11

"I was an only child growing up," John told me, "didn't make a lot of friends back then namely because I graduated high school when I was five."

"Wow, are you serious?" I replied.

"Yeah."

"You must be a genius."

"I'll say, I have an I.Q. of two hundred."

"Funny, you were in high school while I was learning how to walk."

"That's nothing to be ashamed of. Anyway, people had always told me that I was destined for greatness. But after I graduated from college at age nine, everything changed. My parents and I were leaving our apartment, when the unthinkable happened. We saw a giant shadow on the ground, but nothing was casting it! As we stared at it, it started to get bigger, and bigger, and bigger. Until the craziest thing happened, a giant dragon flew out of the ground!"

I gasped. "A dragon?! Oh my, what did it do next?"

"It circled in the air a few times, damaging a lot of the surrounding buildings in the process. Then it landed in the middle of the street. After that, it ran towards us. We tried to run, but it caught up to us in a matter of seconds. It crushed my parents with it's claws, then it tried to burn me. But just when I thought things couldn't get any stranger, I saw a flash of lightning surrounding me, and a sword materialized in my hand. The next thing I knew was after the smoke cleared, the dragon clawed me into a wall, causing me to morph in to a puddle of water for the first time."

"Oh my gosh. How did you escape?"

"I don't know, I must've passed out after the dragon clawed me. Because after that, I woke up in a dark room with four people. One of them greeted me by name, then he walked up to me and explained everything. He told me I was a Guardian, a being with elemental powers, and it was my duty to hunt down the monsters called Darksiders. Having nowhere else to go, I joined them. For the next five years I grew stronger and stronger, until I reached the rank of Guardian Prime at fourteen years old."

"Guardian Prime, What's that?"

"It's the highest rank a Guardian can get, reserved for only the most powerful. Unfortunately most Guardian Primes don't stay in the group after that, they either try to take over or leave it. I chose to stay. I was later assigned to North Star to carry out solo missions for the next four years. Then one day, as I was heading towards the uptown area on my daily routine. I heard the sound of two girls having a little chat."

"You mean May and me?"

"Bingo. I wanted to know what you two were talking about, so I decided to get a closer look. And when I did, I waited for an opportunity to speak, and when it came, I seized it. You know what happens next right?"

"Yeah, I do. But when you left, why did you lie to us?"

John paused for a moment, then he said, "Because I didn't want you involved."

"Really?"

"Yeah, really. Now then, do you have any questions?"

"Yes, how do you turn into water?"

"I told you, I morph. Now let me show you." And then he stood up, took a few steps, turned around, and said, "Stand up Margaret, and I want you to hit me as hard as you can."

As I stood up, I asked John, "Are you sure about this?"

"Of course I'm sure, you'll see."

"Alright, don't say I didn't warn you." And then I leaned back, and punched him with all my weight. But when I did, my fist went right through him, like I hit a water spout. Then I fell to the ground, with my right hand feeling slightly wet.

After that, John looked at me and said, "See, what did I tell you?"

As he helped me to my feet, I looked at him and said, "Ha, ha, very funny. Do all Guardians morph into water like you do?"

"Of course not, in fact that's the least of what I can do. Each Guardian has a different type of element they can use, in my case, I'm a water type."

"Wow, how many types are there?"

"Several, but just to name a few. There are fire, water, wind earth and lightning types. These five elements are considered to be the main element types, if I may."

"But what about metal, lava and ice."

"Metal is a type of earth, and a powerful one at that. Lava is a combination of earth and fire. But as for ice, there's technically no such thing as an ice type."

"Why?"

"Because it's frozen water, therefore it's a type of water."

"I see. Now what about this sword you mentioned, what is it?"

"I'll just have to show you." Then he stretched out his right hand. And with a snap of his wrist, a silver sword flashed into his hand. "This is Thundercloud, the sword that saved my life."

"Woah!"

"Yeah, that's what I thought when I first saw it."

"How did it do that?"

"It's a Guardian Blade, it's supposed to do that."

"I meant how?"

"That I don't know. Guardian Blades have been used by Guardians for centuries. However, not all Guardians can use them, heck most of them don't even need one, understand?"

"I guess I do."

After I said that, John made Thundercloud disappear with another flash. Then he said, "You know Margaret, I should be explaining all this to Percy right now."

"Percy? What does he have to do in all this?"

"Sit down and I'll tell you." After I sat down on the bed, John said, "The day after we met, my superiors told me they had reason to believe that one of the students at North Star High was a potential Guardian, and that they wanted me to investigate. So to avoid suspicion, they got me a job as a note taker the night before so I could keep tabs on everybody. But when I walked into the first class, I never thought I'd see you again."

"Funny, I felt that same way about you."

"Oh really?"

"Yeah."

"Well that's good to know. Anyway, the bottom line is, I believe Percy's that potential Guardian."

"Why him? How do you know it's not somebody else?"

"Because he's gaining weight at an unnatural rate."

"How much weight are you talking about?"

"Twenty-five pounds a week. And like it or not that makes him an earth type."

"Oh my."

"Yeah, is he doing anything tomorrow?"

"He's taking May to the winter prom."

"That's bad Margaret."

"Why, what's wrong?"

"How would you feel if he accidently crushed her?"

"Crushed her?! Oh no, you're not serious are you?"

"I'm dead serious."

"What are we going to do?"

"Tonight, we're not doing anything. Tomorrow on the other hand, I'm taking you home."

"What?! Why?"

"One, because your parents are probably worried sick about you, and two, I need to do something that I'm not allowed to do."

"What's that?"

"Say, 'I'm sorry.'"

"What for?"

"For what happened two months ago."

"Why? Won't you get in trouble?"

"I might but, I want to because I care about you. If anything were to happen, I'd never forgive myself."

When he finished speaking, John closed his eyes and frowned. And as he stood there, I smiled and said, "Well I forgive you."

After that, John looked at me with a weak smile. Then he patted me on the head and replied, "Thank you Margaret. I couldn't have asked for a better friend." And then he grabbed his jacket off the hook, sat down in the armchair, and said, "You can sleep in the bed."

"Okay then, good night John."

"Good night Margaret, see you in the morning."

"Alright." And then he leaned back and wrapped his jacket around his arms, while I hung up my tie, kicked off my shoes, and climbed into bed. A few minutes later, John said something that surprised me, "It's Silverheart."

"Hmm?"

"My last name... It's Silverheart."

"Silverheart... It's a pretty name." And that was the last thing I said for the night. When I fell asleep a few minutes later, I dreamed about Mr. Right.

Like all the previous dreams I had of him, he had a blank face, and it stayed that way for most of the dream. Until it got to the part where we had dinner together. Then he said, "Cover your eyes Margaret."

"Why?" I asked him.

"I'm going to show you my face." Without another question, I covered my eyes. Then a moment later, I heard him say, "You can look now." And when I did, I couldn't believe it. It was John's face, the same blond hair, the same blue eyes, and the same weak smile he had before I went to bed. "What do you think?" he asked in John's voice, and then I woke up.

12

I jumped up and shouted, "John!" And as I sat there in John's bed, I realized it was all a dream, and a very strange one at that. I had always wondered what Mr. Right's face looked like, but I never thought it would look like John's. So what does it mean, he's Mr. Right? How could I know? Anyway, I decided to get up and head to the bathroom.

But when I walked in, John was standing in front of the sink, with his face half shaved, half covered in shaving cream and a razor in his right hand. "Morning Bright Eyes," he said to me.

"Good morning John," was my response, "What time is it?"

"Almost five o' clock."

"Five o'clock?! Wow, did you sleep well last night?"

"I slept like a log. What about you?"

"Surprisingly well."

"Good, then why were you talking in your sleep?"

"I was, talking?" I said with my left eye twitching.

"Yeah, you must've been having a dream or something. Wanna talk about it?"

"No, it was just a dream."

"I see," John said as he continued shaving, "if you need to wash your face or anything, I'll be done in a minute. There's a spare toothbrush if you need to brush your teeth, it's never been opened so it's fine."

"Okay, thank you."

"Hey, what are friends for?" And then I walked out of the bathroom.

After he finished shaving, John left the bathroom so I could wash my face and brush my teeth in peace. After I did those things, I went back to the living room to put on my tie, shoes and jacket. "So, are you taking me straight home?" I asked John.

"That's the plan," was his response.

"But it's still five o' clock in the morning. And by the time we get to my house, we'll still be early."

"So what are you saying, we should take a detour?"

"Well no, I-." before I could say another word, my stomach growled.

"Oh, you're hungry. Why didn't you just say so in the first place? I know a great restaurant not too far from here, it should be open by the time we get there. Wanna go?"

"Sure, why not?" I said to him, and then we left his room. As we walked downstairs, I looked at John and asked him, "What kind of restaurant is it?"

"It's a coffee shop," he told me, "You can get a muffin or two there."

"Good, 'cause for a second there I thought you were taking me to some cheap doughnut shop or something."

"And why would you think that?"

"Well considering the state of your room…"

"Wait, what's wrong with my room?!"

"I'm only kidding," I said while laughing," Your room's fine!"

John let out a sigh of relief, then he looked at me and said with a smile, "Don't scare me like that kid."

"Now how many times have I told you not to call me that?"

"At least a dozen times now, kid."

"Oh you're hopeless." And then we reached the lobby laughing.

As we walked towards the front door, the man from yesterday stood up from his desk and said, "Morning Snake Eyes, going out today?"

"Looks like it Alex," John replied, "I'll be back later tonight."

"Oh I see, you spending some time with your girlfriend?"

"What?! She's not my-!"

"Relax, I'm kidding. She told me that last night, along with a few other things."

"Such as?"

"Nothing really, just your real name, that's all." Before John could respond to that, Alex told him, "Don't worry, I'm not going to tell anybody. Heck, you'll always be Snake Eyes to me."

"Alright, thanks!"

"No problem, now play nice you two!"

"Give me a break!" And then we left The Drunken Turtle.

A mile and a half later, John and I stopped for a moment. Then he stretched out his right arm and pointed towards a building saying, "There it is, right there."

And as I looked in the direction he was pointing in, I saw what it was. It was the restaurant he told me about earlier. It was called, "Hoshi's."

"John it's gorgeous!" I told him, and in my opinion it was. It had green awnings, green leathery material on the seats, and the wood inside looked brand new.

"Well, if you think it looks great from the outside," John said to me, "Then you're gonna love it on the inside. Shall we go in?"

"Oh lets!" And then we walked in.

As we went inside, I saw what John meant. It did look better on the inside. But when we got to the front counter, we saw Jared from school standing behind it wearing a green uniform. "Well if it isn't Margaret Koorikage and Mr. Identity Crisis," he said with a smile, "what can I do for you two?"

"Jared," I said to him, "I didn't know you worked here."

"Yep, every weekend and all through the summer. Now, what can I do for you?"

"Well," John said, "I would like a blue berry muffin and a cup of Joe."

"White or black?" Jared asked him.

"The usual."

"Black it is then." After that, he turned towards me and asked, "And what would you like Margaret?"

"Um," I said while scanning the menu, "I would like a cup of coke and a few cinnamon muffins."

"How many?"

"Uh… Four?"

Right after I said that, John's eyes widened. Then he asked Jared, "How much is this gonna cost?"

"It's not expensive," Jared replied, "But the muffins are pretty big. So I don't think she'll be able to-." Before he could say another word, my stomach growled again.

"You were saying?"

"Never mind." Jared replied, as John handed him the money, then he took us to our seats.

Jared picked a small table by the window. And as we sat down, I asked him, "So, are you going to the winter prom tonight?"

"Can't, I don't have a date."

"And why don't ya?" John said to him.

"Because Margaret didn't want to be my date."

"Oh really, a class act like you?"

"I kinda wondered why for a while. But now that I see you, I understand."

"It's not like that Jared," I told him.

"Sure it is, that's what they always say. Now if you two love birds will excuse me, I need to go back to the counter."

"Alright, do what you have to do then."

"Okay, your food will be ready in a couple of minutes, don't go anywhere!" And then he went back to the counter.

Like Jared said, a few minutes later, our food was ready. He also wasn't kidding about the muffins, they were big! But I somehow managed to eat all four of mine, and as I finished the last one, John gave me a wide eyed stare and said, "You have, quite an appetite for a girl."

"Sorry, I didn't have dinner last night."

"Gee, I wonder why. How was your food?"

"It was delicious, thank you."

"You're welcome, it was my pleasure. Are you ready to go now?"

"I think so."

"Just a second!" said Jared out of the blue, "Could you guys do something for me?"

"Sure," I said as I got up, "what is it?"

Jared pulled out a camera and said, "Smile lovebirds!" Then the next thing I knew, John wrapped his right arm around me, tilted his head to the left, and smiled, while I started to blush. After Jared took the picture, he smiled and said, "Voila, happy customers!"

"Why you- ugh!"

"Woah, calm down! It's nothing personal, we just take pictures of our satisfied customers to remember them. That, and I thought you two looked cute together, made me want to take a picture. So no hard feelings?"

I paused for a moment, then I took a deep breath and said, I suppose not."

"Great, then I hope you don't mind if I send the picture to-."

"And on that note we'll be going now." John said before he could finish his sentence, and then we walked out.

As we walked down the sidewalk, I shouted, "Ugh! The nerve of you! That was probably the most embarrassing thing that ever happened in my life!"

John paused for a moment, then he looked at me and said, "So did you have a good time?"

"Yes, I did." I said with a smile.

"Good, now how much further is your house from here?"

"Just another mile or two."

"Oi."

"Hey, you wanna jog?"

"Jog, why would I wanna do that?"

"Think about it, we could use the exercise, it'll be great! What do you say?"

He paused for a moment, then he smiled and said, "Alright, lead the way."

"Okay," I said as I got in front of him, "just try to keep up."

"Believe me, that's not gonna be a problem." And then we ran the rest of the way home.

13

John and I made it to my neighborhood in an hour or two. And as we stopped to catch our breath, John said, "Gosh, where did you get all that energy?"

"Four cinnamon muffins," was my response, "and for the record, I did tell you to keep up."

"Heh, guess I shouldn't have underestimated you, eh?"

"Well that's a bit of an understatement." And then we started to laugh.

After that, we decided to walk the rest of the way. Then a few steps later, John asked me, "So which house is it?"

"It's on Sixton Street, the third house on the left."

"Could you be a little more specific?"

"Sure, my house number is five 'o eight."

"That's not what I meant Bright Eyes."

"I know, but it's not that much different from the other houses. Except that it's white and it has a black roof."

"Oh really?"

"Yeah, and it's got a swing on the front porch, along with a few bushes and a swing set in the back yard."

"Alright, that shouldn't be too hard to miss. Plus, it sounds nice."

"Thanks, it looks nice too."

"I'll believe that when I see it." Then he stopped and said, "Speaking of which, isn't that your house over there?"

As I looked to where he was pointing, I smiled and said, "Yes, it is."

"Wow, you weren't kidding about it looking nice. Shall we go now?"

"Yes sir." And then we walked towards my house. But as we got to the front door, I said to John as he was about to knock on it, "Wait, don't."

"Why, what's wrong?"

"I didn't come home last night, John, what are my parents going to think? They're already planning to put me on medication, so who knows what they're going to do to me after this?" Then I wrapped my arms around John and said, "John I'm scared!"

And as I cried on his chest, John hugged me and said, "Don't worry about it, you'll be just fine."

"B-but what if they hate me?"

"Come on, they're your parents. How could they possibly hate a sweet girl like you?"

"Thank you but, how do you know they're not going to do something to me?"

He paused for a moment, then he held me tighter and said, "I don't, just cross your fingers and hope for the best, alright?"

I continued to cry for a moment, then I looked at him and said with a smile, "Th-thank you, I-I'll try."

"Good," John said to me, then he wiped off my tears and said, "now will you please stop crying? Pull it together already."

"A-alright, let's do this!" And then I knocked on the door.

A few minutes later, Dad walked out of the front door, then he looked at me and said, "Margaret, where the devil have you been?!"

"Dad look, I can explain. I-!"

"Don't talk! You can tell it to the judge." After that, he turned towards John and asked him, "Who the heck are you?!"

"I'm John Smi-uh-Silverheart sir, and I'm here to apologize."

"Apologize for what?"

"For everything," John told him, "for the damages on the news, the monster sightings, and what happened at Boswell Manor two months ago."

"Alright, explain." And then John told him everything.

He started with the damages and the monster sightings, about how monsters were the ones responsible for the damages, and it was his job to stop them before they became a threat. And about what happened at Boswell Manor and how I was telling the truth about what happened. Then he wrapped it all up by telling dad about the letter and why I didn't come home last night. "And that's what happened sir, I'm truly sorry. Will you please forgive me?"

"I see," Dad told him, "as fascinating as that sounds, there's no way on earth I'll ever believe such a story."

"I had a feeling you'd say that. Then I guess I'll just have to-."

"However, I believe you made it up to cover one small thing."

"Which is?"

Dad paused for a moment, then he grabbed my right arm and shouted, "You've been sleeping with my daughter, haven't you?!"

After that, John's face turned white and sweaty. "Why, no... I never! You've got to believe me, I-!"

"No excuses! I think you've worn out your welcome Mr. Silverheart, good bye and good riddance." And then he dragged me inside.

As he took me to my room, I cried out and begged him to let me go. And when we got to my room, Dad let go of my arm and slapped my face so hard I fell to the floor. Then he walked out and locked the door from the outside. When I got to my knees, I put my hands on my lap and started to cry. Dad never yelled at me like that before and he never had to slap me like that either. All of a sudden, I felt like I didn't know my father at all. What's going on? A few minutes later, I heard a splash on the roof. Then, I saw John crouching on the roof and knocking on my window. After I got to my feet, I walked over to where he was, then I opened the window and said, "John, how did you get up here?"

"I'm a water type Guardian," he said as he climbed into my room, "I can do more than splatter all over the ground." After he did that, I closed the window behind him, then I started to cry again. "Margaret, what's wrong?"

"You know what's wrong," I told him, "Dad accused us of sleeping together. Why would he do that?"

"Well I did ask you to meet me at my hotel room, and you did spend the night with me there."

"Yeah, but you and I both know we didn't sleep together, right?"

"Right."

"So why would he assume that we did? It doesn't make sense."

"I guess not, what do you think he's going to do to you?"

"I don't know. He'll probably transfer me to an all-girls school to keep me away from boys, and he could prevent me from talking to boys too. And he could also... Oh John, what are we going to do?!" And then I threw my arms around John and cried on his chest.

And like before, John hugged me softly and said, "I don't know, but I wouldn't worry about it if I were you. He is your father after all. And if he does anything, he's going to do it because he loves you. Understand?"

I paused for a moment, then I squeezed him tighter and said, "Thank you John, You're a real friend."

"All of a sudden, I feel so welcome." And then we let go of each other, and sat down on my bed.

A few minutes later, John asked me, "Margaret?"

"Yeah?"

"Did you tell anyone about what happened at Boswell Manor?"

"Only my dad and... and Dan Smith."

"WHAT?!"

"I'm sorry, he practically squeezed it out of me."

"Margaret, you've gotta get outta here, NOW!"

"Why?"

"He's not an investigator!"

"Oh no!" I said with a gasp, "Then who is he?"

"He's-."

Before John could say anything, someone kicked down the door. And when we turned to see who it was, we saw Dan Smith standing in the doorway with his dark sunglasses, a wiley grin and clean shaven face saying, "He's right here!"

After that, John lunged at him with Thundercloud in hand. But he dodged it and landed two solid blows to John's right side, causing him to fall to the ground. And as he tried to get up, John said to Dan, "What do you want from me?!"

"You know what I want!" Dan said before he stomped on John, "I want my sword back!"

"If you want it, come and get it!" And then John jumped up, turned to face him, and shot a water ball out of his left hand.

But Dan deflected it with his right arm, then he lunged at John and landed a haymaker to his forehead, knocking him downstairs with a splash. And as he was about to follow, Dad got in front of him saying, "Mister Smith, what is going on?"

Dan responded by punching the side of his face and shouting, "Beat it doofus!" then continued on his way.

As Dad lay on the floor, I ran over to him saying, "Daddy! Oh Daddy, are you okay?!"

"I'm fine sweetheart." He told me, "I've been hit harder than that."

"Where's Mom and Sakura?"

"They went to a birthday party for one of Sakura's friends." Then he pointed downstairs and said, "But if I were you, I'd be more worried about your friend down there."

And when I looked in the direction he was pointing, I saw Dan holding John up by his jacket. Then he threw him towards the kitchen and followed him in that direction. After that, I went downstairs to see what was happening. And when I did, I saw Dan stretching out his right arm saying, "Come to me Thundercloud, Come to your master!" And then he flexed his wrist and shot lightning out of his right hand.

John used Thundercloud to block his attack, but when he did, it looked like Thundercloud was being pulled away from him. John was starting to lose his grip, then Thundercloud flashed out of John's hand and into Dan's. After that, Dan pointed it at John and started to electrocute him. But before he could do that, I ran up to him and grabbed his trench coat shouting, "Stop it! Stop it! Leave him alone!"

And then he stopped electrocuting John... Only to turn around and bash me in the head with the end of the sword's hilt, causing me to fall to the ground and slide into unconsciousness.

14

When I woke up, I was in an abandoned water pump, handcuffed to a plastic pipe and gagged with a white headband. I also noticed a band aid on the right side of my fore head, the same place I got hit. And as I tried to look at it, Dan Smith walked up to me and said, "You're lucky I didn't break your skull open, next time you might not be so lucky."

I replied with a muffled, "What are you going to do to me?"

"Nothing, you see that pipe you're cuffed to? I painted it to look like rusty metal before I did. So when your boyfriend shows up, I'll threaten to fry you if he tries any funny business. And when

I've got him right where I want him, I'll finish him off. Get the picture?"

"You'll never get away with this."

"Watch me." And then I started to cry. "Oh please, will you stop crying?" I didn't stop, then he slapped my face and said, "Stop crying." I couldn't, then he slapped me harder and shouted, "Stop crying!" I still couldn't, then he hit me even harder shouting, "Stop crying!" And after that, he grabbed my face and said, "Stop! Now look at me," Then he took off his sunglasses. His eyes were glowing bright blue, like fire. That must've been the reason he wore sunglasses! "I'm not going to kill you. But I'm going to make your life so miserable, you'll wish I had. Get the picture?"

"Leave her alone you monster!" said John from behind him.

"So," Dan said as he turned to face him, "you got my invitation after all."

"Let her go Smith! Or should I call you by your real name, Kazuki Carlos?"

"Ha, so you finally figured it out..."

"Why?" John said as he got closer to him, "Why go through all this trouble just to get Thundercloud?"

"Because I need it to take over the Guardians Guild."

"Then why were you pretending to be an investigator for the news?"

"Because someone needed to investigate the crime. And that pea-brained reporter believed every word I said to him."

"Where is he?"

"Probably dead, I fried him after I blew up his news van."

"Why?"

"Because if he got in too deep, he'd ruin everything. Get the picture?"

"Quit stalling! Let Margaret go or I'll-!"

"Hold it." Kazuki told him, then he pointed at me and said, "You see your girlfriend over there? She's handcuffed to a metal pole, and what do you think will happen if I were to hit it with one of my lightning bolts? Why, she'd light up like a Christmas tree."

I tried to shout, "No John, it's a trap! It's a trap!" But I couldn't get the words to come out with the gag on.

When John heard my muffled warning, he glared at Kazuki and said, "If you lay one finger on her…"

"You'll do what, eh? Don't you know anything about element types? Fire beats wind, water beats fire and lightning beats water. Get the picture?" Then Kazuki put his arms behind his back and said, "Of course if you show me how much you care about her, maybe I'll let her go." With that being said, John got on his hands and knees. "Is that really how much you care about her?" John nodded his head in agreement, then Kazuki summoned Thundercloud saying, "Then my answer is no." And he tried to hit John with it. John dodged it by rolling to the right, then he got back on his feet and ran behind one of the giant water vats surrounding the inside of the building. "Stay put," Kazuki said as he went after him, "I'll be up on the catwalk, don't move!" Then he ran towards the nearest ladder.

I was left alone now, so I decided to slide down to the ground so I could sit there. Then I put my chin on my chest and cried. "Is this why you kept it a secret?" I thought to myself, "You didn't want me to get hurt, didn't you John? You wanted to protect me. But now it looks like there was no preventing this. Dad, Mom, May... I'm so sorry."

"What the-?!" Kazuki shouted from the catwalk, and then I saw him get hosed by John. John almost pushed him off the catwalk, then Kazuki grabbed the railings shouting, "No more games!" Then he shot lightning out of Thundercloud and said as it brought John to his knees, "Time to end this!!" And then he charged at John, jumped up and hit him with everything he had.

But when he did, there was a blinding flash along with a clanging sound, then the next thing I saw was Kazuki flying through the air. He hit the roof and fell into one of the water vats. With Kazuki gone, I turned towards John. He was holding a black and red sword that looked very familiar, but completely different from Thundercloud. "I... I did it." John said quietly as the sword disappeared, and then he fell off the catwalk and hit the ground with a splash.

When that happened, I jumped up, somehow managed to break the handcuffs in half, tore off the gag and ran towards him saying, "Oh no, John! John! John!!" And when I got to where he was, I fell to my knees, then I put my hands in the puddle and started to look for him. As I did that, I noticed I was holding Thundercloud backwards in my right hand. "How did you get in my hand, am I a Guardian?" Then I hit the ground to see if anything happened. Nothing did. "Guess not." I told myself, then I saw a bubble come up from the side of the puddle. "John? Are you alright?" He didn't respond, then I put my left hand a little further away from the bubble and said, "John, if you can hear me, grab my hand." He still didn't respond. "Please?" I waited for a minute or two to see if he'd do anything, but nothing happened. "No, John…" But just as I was about to give up, I felt him grab my hand. Then I pulled him out and said, "John, are you alright?"

"I am now." John replied, "You?" I responded by nodding my head, then he looked down and asked me, "Why are you holding Thundercloud?"

"I don't know."

"Neither do I. Only a Guardian can wield a Guardian blade, so you shouldn't be able to touch it let alone hold it in your hand like that."

"So what do you think it is?"

"I think it's a mystery." And then Thundercloud disappeared.

"And what about the other one?"

"What other one?"

"The other Guardian blade, what do think that was?"

John paused for a moment, then he told me, "I have absolutely no idea."

After that, I threw my arms around John, then I said as I cried on his chest, "You were trying to protect me all along. I'm so sorry, I shouldn't have invaded your privacy like that. I just-."

"No," he said as he hugged me back, "I'm the one who should apologize. You've been the best friend I ever had, and how do I repay you? By lying to your face. I'm so sorry!"

"Oh John!" And then we hugged each other even tighter.

A few minutes later, John said to me softly, "I've gotta go now Bright Eyes. Your Dad's waiting for you outside, you should go to him."

"Alright John, please be careful."

"I will."

"And John…"

"Yeah?"

"Thank you for rescuing me."

"Aw Margaret, it was the least I could do." And then he grabbed the broken handcuffs on my wrists, squeezed them until they clicked and fell off, then he ran towards one of the ladders, while I walked out through one of the doors.

As I left the building, I saw Dad's car parked out in front of it. And as I got close enough to it, Dad ran towards me saying, "Margaret, oh my gosh Margaret!"

"Daddy, Daddy!" And then I jumped into Dad's arms.

"Thank goodness you're alright, did he hurt you?"

"I'm fine, he didn't hurt me too badly."

Dad looked at me for a moment, then said, "At least that thug had the decency to bandage you."

"Dad, can we please leave now? I wanna go home."

"Of course sweetheart, let's go home." And then we walked to the car.

But as we did, Dad and I heard a crash from the building. Then we turned around and saw John riding on a river of water from rooftop to rooftop. "Do you believe me now?" I said to Dad.

"With all my heart," he told me, and then we got in the car and drove home.

15

The next day, I found out May was in the hospital. Apparently her left foot got run over by a semi-truck after she and Percy left the winter prom, but when my family and I went to visit her, she told me a different story. "The truck didn't break my foot, Percy did." She told me, "He accidently stepped on it after he saved me from the truck. Some hero, am I right?"

"Right," was my response, "but why didn't you tell them it was Percy?"

"I was about to, but then I decided to let everyone think it was the truck. 'Cause I mean, who'd believe Percy crushed my foot after he stopped a semi-truck with his bare hands?"

I paused for a moment, then I told her, "After what happened yesterday, I would."

"Why, what happened?"

"It's a long story…" Then I told her what happened the day before and the night before that.

When I finished, May grabbed my shirt and said, "WHAT?! Why didn't you tell me about it sooner?!"

"I wanted to, but I didn't think you'd believe me."

"Of course I would Margaret," May said as she let go of my shirt, "you're my best friend remember?"

"But I thought-."

"Yeah, about the whole, 'our friendship is over' thing. I'm sorry, I didn't mean what I said. Will you please forgive me?"

I paused for a moment, then I said with a smile, "Of course I do May, what are best friends for?" And then we hugged each other.

A little while later, some students from our school came by to see how May was doing. They were very nice, they even wanted to talk to me and see how I was doing. More students came after them, and before I knew it, it turned into a get well soon party for May. As more and more people showed up, Jared came by and handed me an envelope saying, "It's the picture of you and John from yesterday, open it and see how it turned out."

And when I did, I couldn't help but smile. It turned out beautifully, John had his arm around me and was smiling, while

I looked like I was about to die of embarrassment. "Thank you," I told him, "it's gorgeous."

"I figured you'd say that, so I made you two copies. One for you and one for your boyfriend."

"I'll make sure he gets it," I said with a chuckle.

"Ooh, ooh! Can I see it?" said May from her bed.

And that's why I'm here today, at the park in front of the fountain, one week after that day. It was two 'o clock in the afternoon when I decided to meet John here, and I was starting to get worried that he wasn't going to come. Then just as I was about to go look for him, John came up to me and said, "Hey Bright Eyes."

"Hi John!" I replied, "Did you get my note?"

"I did, you said you wanted to give me something. What is it?"

"It's the photo Jared took of you and me, he made us copies of it. Here's yours."

After I handed him the photo, he looked at it for a moment. Then he put it in his wallet and said with a smile, "I'll treasure it always. But something tells me you wanted to see me for more than just a photo."

"Yes, how's Percy?"

"He's fine. But after what happened last week, his relationship with May has gotten a little 'rocky,' if you know what I mean."

"Oh, I do. So what's going to happen to him?"

"He's going to learn how to control his power. It'll take some time, but he'll get the hang of it."

"And what about you?"

"Me? I'll be going back to my usual routine, nothing special."

"Could you stop by and see me every now and then?"

"Sure, why not? We're friends aren't we?"

"We are."

"Yep." And then we remained silent for a moment.

Then a few minutes later, I said, "John?"

"Yeah?"

"Do you remember when we first met?"

"I remember it like it was yesterday."

"I wanted to meet here because I thought it'd be better than that alley, remember?"

"Oh yes, much better."

"You know, this reminds me of our friendship."

"What does?"

"Being here at the park with you. When I think back to where we first met, our friendship was a lot like that alley, dirty and undesirable. Now it's become clean and beautiful like the fountain over there."

"You forgot wet, Margaret." Then we started to laugh. After that, John looked at me and said, "Oh, speaking of friendship. I've got something to give you too."

"Really, what is it?"

"Close your eyes and you'll find out."

After I shut my eyes, I asked John, "Okay, what is it?" And then he grabbed the back of my head, and kissed me on my right cheek. After he did that, I opened my eyes and said as my cheeks turned red, "Why, John! You-."

"Relax, I'm not gonna make a habit out of this. In fact, I did that because I'm saving the lips for later. Do you understand Margaret?" I didn't breathe a word, then I heard the distant sound of church bells ringing. "Would you look at the time? I've gotta go now, duty calls and all that. See you later Bright Eyes." Then he ran out of the park.

As he did that, I put my hand on my cheek. Then I smiled and said, "Good bye… Mr. Right." And then I watched him run off into the distance.

Thomas J. Mohr is an aspiring writer, doodler, manga fanatic and occasional Shakespearian from Bostwick Fl.

Suffering from Autism, ADHD, Anxiety, Germ phobia and two hardheaded brothers, he developed a passion for telling stories at fourteen and writing comics at seventeen. Now if only he were like that with his homework...

Copyright Thomas J. Mohr © 2016

Made in the USA
Charleston, SC
29 February 2016